I CAME TO BRING THE PAIN

ROY GLENN

I CAME TO BRING THE PAIN

BY

ROY GLENN

ROY GLENN

I CAME TO BRING THE PAIN

1

"Are you listening to me, Nick?" Monika asked.

"No. I'm sorry. My mind was someplace else," Nick said.

"As usual."

"What did you say?"

"It's not important. But I need you here—with me, Nick. And I need you to be focused on what we're doing," Monika said, and Nick knew that she was right.

They had been in Sana'a, Yemen for over a month and had finished the work on the oil company contract weeks ago, but this was the first opportunity they'd had to complete their objective.

Take Boko Mansur, a high-value target in Al-Shabab, into custody and turn him over to the Kenyan authorities or kill him. Intelligence sources reported that Mansur was in Sana'a to join up with the Al Qaeda militants operating in the country.

Mansur was staying at a place called the Villa In Hadda. Reconnaissance of the property and the area surrounding it made it much more feasible to get them moving into an ambush. In her first field op, Carla was assigned to switch phones with Mansur and keep him occupied while Monika planted a tracker in his phone.

But from the start, the mission had been compromised because of these words: *I think we did have sex that night, Nick. And I think you are my son's father.* Since he'd heard those words, Nick hadn't been the same because he was so distracted.

To make matters worse, Black had called Monika and told her that he needed her and Nick home. Monika explained the situation and then she made him a promise.

"I'll be there as soon as I can."

When she explained what was happening to Nick, all he could do was shake his head.

"Must be serious," he said and thought that it couldn't be happening at a worse time.

Throughout his life, Nick had never given any thought to being a father. In fact, it was something that he wasn't interested in at all.

When Nick was eleven, his parents disappeared. They just didn't come home one night. Unwanted by his uncle and aunt, he was separated from his younger brother and sister and sent to live with his grandmother. After she died, Mike Black, Bobby Ray, Wanda Moore, Perry Dukes, Vickie Payne, and Jamaica became Nick's family.

And now to find out that not only did he have a son, but that the boy was sixteen years old, was mind boggling to say the least. There was no question about it, Nick had a son and his name was Marvin. And he owed having that information to Colonel Mathis.

The only person Nick told was the colonel. Nick was noticeably quiet during the briefing and that fact did not escape the attention of the colonel. "What's bothering you, son?" When Nick was finished Mathis stopped and looked at him. "Maybe I can help with that."

Ten days later, the colonel made an unannounced visit to Yemen. "I need to speak with you alone, Captain," he said. And that was enough to clear the room.

"What can I do for you, Colonel?" Nick asked after the rest of the team left the room.

"This time I did something for you,' the colonel said and handed Nick an envelope.

Nick looked at the envelope and then at the colonel. "What's this?"

"Open it."

Nick opened the envelope and read its contents. "How did you get this?"

"I sent a team to infiltrate and acquire the information."

Nick laughed. "You're kidding."

"Oh yeah, high-priority op. My team infiltrated the cafeteria at the boy's school. When he dropped off his lunch tray, we had his DNA. You know we have yours. The rest was easy." The colonel stepped closer to Nick and extended his hand. "Congratulations, son. You're the father of a sixteen-year-old boy."

It wasn't easy, but Nick had to wait to talk to April about it. It was Tuesday at eight AM in Sana'a and that meant that it was midnight on Monday in New York. After waiting over nine hours, Nick dialed April's number at the office.

"April Dancer," she sang.

"Good morning, April. It's Nick."

"Oh God, what's wrong now?" April asked and started fumbling with the papers on her desk.

Nick and April had talked every day since the team had been in Sana'a. On some days, the two spoke multiple times and as they usually did, the two butted heads on every point. That was due in large part to the mountain of sexual friction that existed between them. Even though both Nick and April denied it, the tension was obvious to everyone around them.

At the end of the day, everything always worked out because they actually worked well together. However, for Nick and April that meant fighting out everything. When they did finally come together on a solution to whatever the issue was and they got still and quiet enough to step back and admire the work they had done, the look they shared was magical.

The fact was that Nick and April were digging each other; it was written all over both of their faces. The way each looked at the other when they thought the other wasn't looking. From time to time, April slipped into the fantasy she'd created about presenting the project to Black in Freeport instead of Manhattan. That night, she had been thinking about making love to Nick; and it wasn't the first time that those thoughts had consumed April.

In her fantasy they would take a romantic walk on the beach with warm tropical breezes blowing through her hair. Then Nick would walk her to her room and April would invite him in for a nightcap. The two would engage in the same intense conversations that always proved to stimulate more than just her mind. And then, there would be that moment, the window when everything seems right and then Nick would kiss her. Then April would make love to him like she had imagined many times before.

"Did something go wrong with the facial recognition software again?"

"No, April, nothing's wrong."

"Then what do you want? You know I have a staff meeting in five minutes."

"I need to talk to you, so send an e-mail and cancel it," Nick ordered.

"Yes sir, Captain, sir. Your wish is my command, Captain, sir. I am typing just as fast as I can—and—send. There, it's done. Now, what do you want to talk about?"

Even though Nick and April had talked, the one thing that they hadn't talked about was the only thing that both of them wanted to talk about, but neither brought up.

Nick had spent the day thinking about what he would say to her. He even had a little speech prepared. Nick had also spent all day thinking about what him being the father of April's son, Marvin, meant for the future. There were times when Nick would allow himself to think about what it might be like if he were to just be with one woman, and that woman was April. There were times when Nick longed for the type of relationship the Black and Shy have together. Then at other times, Nick wondered why he would ever give up Tasheka, Danielle and Mercedes, or Rain or Wanda for that matter. He liked April—wanted her—but this changed everything.

Now that he finally had April on the phone, Nick couldn't remember one single word of what he was going to say to her. "I wanted to talk to you about our son."

There was silence on the line.

"How do you know that Marvin is really your son?" April finally asked.

"I have the DNA report in my hand."

"How did you get that?"

"You don't wanna know, April."

"Probably has something to do with that creepy Colonel Mathis." April laughed and thought about all of the things that the team had told her about the colonel. Then she got quiet again. "But you're really Marvin's father, Nick?"

"Yes, April, Marvin is definitely our son," Nick said and April was overjoyed to hear the excitement in his voice.

2

When the colonel returned to the briefing room the following morning, Nick wondered what was going on. "Mission has changed, Captain," Mathis began. "We have new intelligence that says Mansur is in fact in country to meet with members of Al-Qaeda, but not to join up with them."

"What's his objective?"

"We believe he is here to receive plans and instructions about a coordinated attack. Which means that the operation just became mission critical and that much harder."

"This changes the entire op."

"It does."

"Why didn't you tell me this yesterday?"

"I thought you needed a day to wrap your mind around being a father," Mathis said.

"You got any kids, Colonel?"

"Two boys and a girl," Mathis said, and then he laid out the new mission parameters for Nick.

On the morning that the operation was to take place, the team dressed in plain clothes and reviewed the plan one last time. "Ride him hard and fast, and take him when he's in the perfect position," Monika said and one by one, the team left to assume their positions.

Then Carla sat down at the console for her first live action mission. "System active. Systems check," she said as all her systems passed their checks. "Sound check."

"Acknowledged, Omega," Xavier said. "You're going to do fine," he said and got out of the van.

"Acknowledged signal, Omega," Travis said and checked his weapon. "You know you got this."

"Beta acknowledging your signal, Omega. Just like we practiced it," Monika said.

"We all know Omega is ready to rock. Now let's clean up this traffic," Nick said.

Carla scanned for the target. "Target is active. Target acquired."

Xavier was parked alongside of Khawlan Street, the only road leading from the villa. He looked around, and then he walked to the front of the van and opened the hood.

"Target is on the move," Carla said.

"Acknowledged, Omega," Monika said. "Beta proceeding with phase one." She looked at Nick. "You ready?"

"Let's go."

Nick and Monika got out of their four-door Toyota Hilux truck and approached a car that was parked near a red light. While Nick looked out, Monika planted an explosive device on the car. Then she planted a second device on another car that was parked three cars from the light. When she was done, Nick walked across the street, got in the Hilux, and drove off.

"Alpha is on the move."

"Acknowledged, Alpha," Carla said.

Monika moved to a safe distance from the cars, took a device from her pocket, and then she waited.

"Target now passing your location, Gamma," Carla said.

"Acknowledged, Omega," Xavier closed the hood, got back in the van, and started it up. "Gamma in pursuit." His job was to maintain pursuit of the target vehicle.

"Target is one point two kilometers from your position, Beta."

"Acknowledged, Omega," Monika said. "Beta is in position and standing by."

As they were anticipating, there was a three-car convoy and they were confident that there would be at least one backup team somewhere nearby.

"Target is five hundred meters from your location."

"Acknowledged. Beta standing by."

As Mansur's convoy approached the light on 48th Street, Monika pressed the button on the device and made the light change to red. When the convoy stopped at the light, Xavier pulled the van close in behind them.

Then Monika pressed the detonator and the parked car exploded. She approached the lead vehicle, pulled the pin, rolled a grenade under the car and quickly moved to a safe distance. When it exploded, Xavier got out of the van. He and Monika opened fire on the remaining two cars in the convoy.

"Get us out of here," Mansur demanded as his driver backed into the car behind it and pulled out. Xavier and Monika continued to fire as both vehicles sped past them.

"Target is out of the box."

"Acknowledged, Omega," Travis said. "Delta is in position."

Xavier ran back to the van and got in. "Acknowledged, Omega. Gamma in pursuit."

When the backup team arrived at the scene, Monika pressed the detonator, and the second parked car exploded near the backup teams' vehicle. Monika engaged them immediately. She fired through the window and took out the driver. One man got out of the backseat and Monika shot him as he prepared to shoot. Then Monika quickly dealt with the third man as he came out of the back door. Once the backup team was taken care of, Monika ran back to her car, started it up and drove off. "Beta in route to choke point."

"Acknowledged, Beta," Carla said. "Target is three hundred meters from your location, Delta."

"Acknowledged. Delta standing by."

Travis moved into position on the side of the road with a grenade launcher and took aim.

"Target in three, two, one. . . "

The target vehicle passed by Travis' position and he fired at the second vehicle. "Pursuit vehicle destroyed." Travis returned to his car, as Xavier sped past his position.

Now only the target vehicle remained.

"Acknowledged, Delta. Proceed to the choke point."

"Acknowledged."

"Omega to Alpha."

"Go ahead with your traffic."

"Target vehicle is one point eight kilometers from your position."

"Acknowledged, Omega," Nick said. "In position." He put on his helmet and harness and waited for the word to go from Carla.

"Target vehicle is three hundred meters from your position."

"Standing by," Nick said.

"Two hundred meters." With his foot on the brake, Nick put the Hilux in drive and stepped on the gas. "Target in five, four, three, two, one. He's yours."

I CAME TO BRING THE PAIN

Nick took his foot off the brake, sped off and rammed the Toyota truck into Mansur's vehicle. Nick got out of the truck with his night vision goggles on, dropped two smoke grenades, took out his weapon and opened fire. When Xavier arrived in the van, he got out of the truck wearing his goggles and opened fire. Then Monika arrived on the scene; she put on her goggles, exited her vehicle and fired.

Mansur's driver and his two bodyguards returned fire as best as they could in the smoke. However, with their night vision goggles on, the team could see just fine, because the goggles could not only produce an image on the darkest of nights, but could see through smoke as well.

Travis arrived on the scene, exited his vehicle and went straight to Mansur's car. Travis opened the back door and pulled Mansur out at gunpoint. Monika fired and hit the driver with two shots, while Nick and Xavier took down the bodyguards. As Mansur struggled, Travis dragged him to the van and got in. Once he had secured Mansur, Travis took the wheel and drove away. The rest of the team moved quickly to the Hilux truck and left the scene.

3

"We're at war now," Black told his captain's that night at Cuisine. "Right or wrong, this is the path that the boss of this family put us on. And like I told Bobby, we're not going to sit down with Brill and try to talk our way outta this. We're definitely not going to sit down with some stupid niggas that Rain got fighting each other. And we got Benitez's people that we gotta deal with."

With Black once again firmly in command of his family and Bobby serving as wartime consigliere, Rain took over running the day-to-day operations. Her job was to run the war while at the same time, keep their businesses up and running. "I know you can handle it, Rain."

"I won't betray the confidence you got in me," Rain said.

"You better not. We already had one person betray us," Bobby said.

Rain knew that he was talking about Wanda. That was a subject that she knew Black wasn't going to talk about; and to be honest, Rain had no desire to talk about it. She never really liked Wanda and strongly objected to what she was doing. Rain was glad she was gone. Her main concern was Lloyd Brill.

When Howard and Sherman told her that Brill, André Harmon and Cazzie Riley tried to kill her father, Rain was furious. She wanted to rush out and kill him, but Black told her no.

"If you think that this is gonna turn into some personal vendetta, I can't use you."

"But—"

"Ain't no but about it. I need you clear headed to do what I need you to do." Black put his hands on her shoulders. "We *are* going to kill Brill, Rain. I promise you that. But since Brill doesn't know it was us, we're gonna hit him when it makes sense."

What Rain didn't know, was that Brill already knew that it was them that had been hitting his operations. The day after the grand reopening of Cuisine, Big Walt McDonald was laid to rest. At the funeral, Brill approached Carolina Royce. She had been dating Big Walt for years.

"I wanted to say that I'm sorry for your loss, Carolina. Big Walt was a good man."

"Thank you, Lloyd."

"You were there that night. Did you get a look at who did it?"

Carolina thought for a minute. She knew exactly who it was that shot Big Walt. She stood and watched as Spence walked up behind Big Walt and killed him. "I saw them."

She liked Spence; and in spite of the fact that he had killed her man, Carolina was unwilling to tell Brill that. "I know it was one of Black's people."

"I promise you, I'll kill the mutha fuckas that did this." Brill walked away. "Is Black even in the country?" he asked one of his men.

"I ain't seen Black, Bobby, or Nick in months."

"Then who's running that crew?"

Not knowing who was sitting at the top of Black's organization, Brill went after the easiest high-value target he could find. Later that night when Sherman was closing up for the night, he came out of the store with Debra. He had just pulled the gate down and put the lock on it, and then he stood up and saw the car coming slowly. Sherman recognized the man in the backseat and knew that he was one of Brill's men.

The gun came out the window.

Sherman took out his gun and looked at Debra. "Run!" he shouted and opened fire on the car.

Brill's man sprayed the storefront with bullets. Once they had passed, Sherman ran out in the street and kept firing at the car until the clip was empty. He turned and looked back for Debra and didn't see her.

"Debra! You a'ight?" But he got no answer.

When Sherman walked back to the store, he saw Debra's body.

She was dead.

After Debra's tragic death, Sherman put new people in place, along with some security, to run the store and keep the number bank running. With that taken care of, Sherman moved to the warehouse where Rain ran one of her father's old gambling spots. From there, he took control of the war at Rain's command. There were other changes made as well. Rain put Howard Owens in charge of keeping the money flowing.

Both Black and Bobby have moved back into the neighborhood. Without their knowledge, Wanda never sold either of their old houses so they were able to move back in. And Smoke was now Bobby's bodyguard.

As the war raged on three fronts, there was still the matter of Lanisha Henderson to deal with. To keep from going to jail for a possession of cocaine charge, FBI agent Fred Dawson, who was trying to build a RICO case against Black, forced her to start wearing a wire when she came in contact with Bobby. Lanisha hated every minute of what she was doing and revealed the wire to Bobby. When Bobby told Black that they had a problem with the FBI, Black only had one question: "You didn't kill her?"

But Bobby knew that something had to be done with her.

When things quieted down a bit, Bobby took Lanisha on a week vacation to the Yahnica Beach Resort & Spa in Aruba. While they were there, Bobby and Lanisha experienced the nightlife. Every night it was someplace different. They went from flashy dance clubs and lounges to laid-back bars. All of the major hotels and resorts in Eagle Beach had posh bars, casinos, and nightclubs. The Marriott Resort was a hot nightlife destination, particularly because of its grand Stellaris Casino.

In addition to partying at the hotels and major resorts, they went to the capital city, Oranjestad, where a large majority of the nightlife is. Places like Carlos and Charlie's Bar—that place was always jumping each time they went there. They had been to Mambo Jambo Café and Escape. There were also party bus tours in Aruba. Their favorite was Bonbini Chiva Paranda.

Later that night when they got back to their room, it didn't take long before clothes were flying everywhere. Bobby attacked her tongue with a vengeance. He squeezed her breasts lightly and took her nipple between his teeth. "Oh yes!"

Bobby pushed her legs open and pinned her up against the wall. Lanisha closed her eyes and Bobby felt her body tremble as he eased a penetrating finger in and out of her.

"That feels so good," Lanisha said softly, and Bobby grabbed her thighs and lifted her off her feet. Before she could catch her breath, Bobby thrust himself into her.

Lanisha rocked her hips, moving her body into his. "Fuck me!"

Bobby thrust himself deep inside her and felt her juices flowing down his thighs. Then he felt her muscles lock as her head drifted back in quiet ecstasy.

Lanisha collapsed on the bed and Bobby sat down next to her. She touched Bobby's face and he ran his hand over her soft skin. She rolled into Bobby's arms and kissed him.

After a while, Lanisha got out of bed and went into the bathroom to take a shower. When she came out of the shower, Lanisha called for Bobby. When he didn't answer, she came out of the bathroom and screamed when she saw Smoke sitting in the chair by the bed with a gun in his hand. He quickly raised his weapon and fired two shots to her chest, and she fell on the bed.

4

While Smoke called for Leon's people to come and cleanup the room, Bobby came back in. He leaned over Lanisha, shook his head, and then he touched her cheek. Bobby took a deep breath and looked at Smoke.

"Make sure it's done right and I'll see you back in New York."

Back in the city, at the warehouse that Sherman now ran the war from, Rain came in and demanded to know what was going on with Jah Staton. He ran the drug operation for Brill.

Sherman looked at his watch. "Ice and Mitch should just be getting there now."

The Dyckman Marina has been a vital part of upper Manhattan's waterfront culture for more than two centuries. Ice and Mitch walked in the newly rebuilt La Marina Restaurant and Lounge, on Dyckman Street. After years of attempts on his life, Jah Staton thought that he was untouchable. For that reason, Jah never traveled with any security. That night, he was about to dig into a steak with a side of shishito peppers when he saw Ice and Mitch.

Staton pulled his gun, opened fire, and ran out the back door with Mitch and Ice right on his ass. He stopped, turned around quickly, and fired a couple of shots at them as they ran out the back door. The shots ricocheted off the door. Mitch and Ice took cover behind the dumpster and returned fire. Staton kept running.

Ice and Mitch immediately took off behind him. "I told you he was gonna run when he saw us," Ice said as he ran.

"I got him. Go get the car," Mitch said and kept going.

Ice turned around and went for the car. Staton looked over his shoulder and could see that Mitch was catching up with him. He turned around quickly and fired. Mitch ducked behind a car. He stayed low while Staton kept firing until he emptied the clip. He started running again and put in a fresh clip.

Ice made it to the car, started up and went to find Mitch. He rounded the corner in time to see Staton run up to a car that was stopped at a red light. Staton pulled the driver out, and then he got in and drove away. Ice went after him just as Mitch caught up.

Ice slowed down a little and watched as Staton, thinking that he had given his pursuers the slip, parked the car and went inside a bar. Ice drove around the corner and parked the car. He called Mitch and told him where he was, and then Ice put the silencer on his gun and then went in after him.

Staton was standing at the bar waiting for the bartender. Ice walked up behind him and Staton felt pressure in the small of his back. "Now we gonna walk up outta here nice and quiet," Ice said.

Ice walked him out of the bar. They went down the street and around the corner, and then Ice walked him into an alley. Ice raised his gun and shot Staton in the head. He put the gun away and took out his cell to call Mitch. He answered on the first ring.

"You get him?"

"I got him."

5

Zack Moreno was involved in drug trafficking, as well as illegal gambling, extortion and prostitution. When Hamilton Dunbar, another of Brill's top men, was murdered on Wanda's orders, Moreno stepped into his position; but Brill never really trusted him. After their death's, Brill found out that Dunbar and Kurt Felder were planning to kill him.

Moreno had been longtime allies with Kevin 'Krush Rock' Felder, Kurt Felder's cousin. He was convinced that if his cousin was plotting against him, then it only stood to reason that Krush Rock and Moreno weren't to be trusted. And Brill was right. They were conspiring to eliminate Brill so they could take power.

They invited Brill to come to a neutral spot, which they said was for his safety. The purpose of the meeting was to talk strategy and plan their next move against Black. At that meeting they planned to assassinate Brill.

Cal Worrell, one of Rain's informants inside of Brill's organization, heard about the plan and called her. "It really is gonna be to your advantage to find out where the ambush is gonna be and let me know," she told her informant. Once he found out the information that Rain wanted he called her.

Now Rain knew the place; but what she didn't know was when. She had Kayo rent an apartment across the courtyard on Pelham Parkway where Moreno and Krush Rock had set their trap. He and Treach had been there for four days and there was no sign of Brill. The plan was to hit Brill as soon as he came in the courtyard and catch Moreno and Krush Rock when they came out of the apartment.

Meanwhile, in the dressing room at Conversations, Lola Luv was getting ready to perform. As they finished her hair and began her makeup, Lola thought about where she was and what she was about to do and felt a little jealous. While Cristal, Monte Cole, and P Harlem were on a ten-city tour, she was stuck in the city playing club dates.

Her real name was Lola Frazier. She was born and raised in the Bronx and lived much of her young life on the streets after being kicked out by her abusive father. In her teens, Lola Luv would rap; heavily influenced by female hip-hop artists like Lil' Kim and Foxy Brown, and singer Whitney Houston. After the success of her three mix tapes, Lola Luv was signed to Big Night Records by Fuller Gordon. Performing with The Regulators got her music career started.

Lola Luv's debut studio album was certified double platinum by the Recording Industry Association of America and spawned three number one hits. Her following albums were certified platinum. She was featured on the single "We Never Stop," which featured other female recording artists, and went to number one on the US Billboard Hot 100. Throughout her career, Lola Luv had earned several accolades for her work.

But that had all been years ago. Lola was twenty-nine now and it had been years since she had a solo track crack the top twenty on the Hot 100. She and her manager sat quietly at the Big Night launch meeting and listened to Gladys Gordon and Meka Brazil layout their vision for the future.

"We will honor all existing contracts. However, going forward, artists will have to come to us with something that is commercially viable."

Lola was told in a private meeting with Gladys, that the company would be focusing their marketing and promotion efforts on Cristal, The Regulators, The One, and P Harlem. "As well as you, Lola," Gladys said.

Lola was also promised that in the coming weeks, Gladys would sit down and meet with Lola and her management to map out their plans for the future. However, to this point, that meeting hasn't taken place. There was always some excuse why either Gladys or Meka had to cancel. Lola assumed the worst.

And to make matters worse, she hadn't seen Kayo in almost a week.

She had met Kayo at the after-party at Impressions on the night that Cuisine reopened. They met again after Lola did a show at Mingles. Kayo was in the house when she performed at The 40/40 Club and they had been together ever since. Lola had gotten a text from him, promising her that he'd be down front at Conversations for the show.

While Lola Luv was made ready to go onstage, back at the apartment on Pelham Parkway, Treach was beginning to get a little restless. "I don't think Brill is gonna show up here. And I'm tired of just sitting here," Treach complained.

"What you wanna do?" Kayo asked.

"I think we should make an executive decision."

"I'm listening."

"There's one man at the gate and one walking the courtyard. We gotta take them first. Then there are two guys in the living room"—Treach looked out the scope in the window—"One more in the kitchen. I say we go in through the window on the back side of the building. We go down the hall and start blastin'."

"When you wanna do it?" Kayo asked.

"I say we hit them now and tell Jackie that we thought they were gettin' ready to move on us, so we hit them first."

"Why?"

"Why what?"

"They are gonna wanna know why they were gettin' ready to come at us," Kayo said. Treach looked confused. "Jackie is gonna wanna know which one of us did something fucked up to let them know we were there."

"I'll say I had some ho's over there and one of them must have told them about us," Treach paused and thought the lie through. "Yeah, Jackie ain't gonna be mad at a nigga 'bout gettin' some pussy."

"Don't hate 'cause she walks more pussy out that club every night than you do."

"I ain't hatin'—just statin' a fact. Jackie ain't gonna be too mad 'bout this shit."

"Especially if we kill Moreno and Krush Rock because of it."

"Exactly. So here's the story: After the bitch left here, I saw her outside talking to one of Moreno's people. She must have told them then."

"So we hit them first. Cool." Kayo looked at his watch. He knew that Lola was getting ready to go onstage. "Let's do it," he said and armed himself.

The houselights at Conversations went down. The music began to get lower and the people who had seats started making their way off the dance floor. By the time the stage lights came up, the floor was crowded again.

"*Good evening, ladies and gentlemen; and welcome to Conversations.*"

The crowd began making noise. The beat started pounding.

"*Please join me in welcoming to the stage, Big Night Recording Artist, Lola Luv!*"

Kayo moved around building and came up behind the man by the gate and took him out. When he went down, Treach spotted the one walking the property and took aim from the window with a Barrett 82A rifle with a silencer. He dropped him with one shot. While he looked out, Kayo moved his body out of sight, and then they went around the side of the building. Once Kayo and Treach got to the window they went in.

Treach went to the door and peeked out into the hallway. "Hallway is clear. You ready to do this?"

"Right behind you," Kayo said.

"I'll take Krush Rock and the one in the living room. Moreno is yours."

"Got it," Kayo said and followed Treach into the hallway.

When they reached the living room, Treach tossed a flash grenade into the room. The blinding flash of light and loud noise disoriented their enemy's senses long enough to gain the advantage. Kayo moved toward the kitchen while

Treach went in the living room. Before he could react, Kayo entered the room and fired two shots. Kayo looked at the dead man; it wasn't Moreno.

Before they could recover from the noise, Treach went in after the two men in the living room. He hit Krush Rock and killed him. Then Treach fired two more shots at the other man and he went down.

Kayo came into the living room and looked at the two men that Treach killed; Moreno wasn't one of them. "We need to find Moreno."

Back at Conversations, the audience erupted into applause when the dancers, who were wearing red latex corsets and red thigh boots, walked out onstage and began to dance. The crowd went wild when Lola hit the stage in a black latex corset and black, custom-made Christian Louboutin Monicarina thigh-high, leather boots and joined the dancers.

Early in her career, Lola never felt the need to wear an outfit, and she never danced. She would walk out onstage wearing whatever she had on that day, grab the mic, and do her work. Now, as she tried to restart her career, Lola had hired a personal trainer to get her in top shape, a costume designer, and a choreographer to teach her how to dance.

With one of her hits playing, Lola danced just as well as any of her dancers before she finally grabbed the mic and put in her work. All the while Lola was performing; she was looking out in the crowd to see if she could spot Kayo.

Treach and Kayo moved through the apartment looking for Moreno and then they heard a noise. Treach ducked in the shadows and Kayo waited in a doorway as a man came out of the room with a gun in his hand and looked around.

Kayo moved out and caught him with two to the back of his head. "That ain't him either."

Kayo centered himself and kicked in the door. Treach went through the door quickly and spotted Moreno in the corner of the room. He opened fire and Treach hit the floor. Kayo came in the room and fired two shots to Moreno's chest, and then one to the head.

After the show was over and Lola took her bows, she scanned the crowd in front of her and looked to her side, and was disappointed that Kayo wasn't there. Lola returned to her dressing room.

"Good show, Lola." Lola thanked the stage manager, but had no time to talk. She rushed to her dressing room thinking that Kayo would be in there waiting for her. She burst through the door and once again was disappointed that Kayo wasn't there.

"Might as well change clothes and go home," a very sad Lola said.

When she was dressed, Lola opened the door and smiled when she saw Kayo standing there with two dozen roses in his hand.

7

After making sure that Black's mother and the children were well protected, Napoleon came back to New York to resume his job as Black's driver. Even though that was his job title, Napoleon knew that he was Black's bodyguard. He also knew that he had a dangerous job.

Napoleon knew Kevon, Black's last bodyguard. They were friends. So when Kevon was killed protecting Black in Freeport, he begged Jamaica to give him the job to honor his friend. However, when Napoleon returned to New York, Black had other plans for him.

"I got a new job for you, but you're gonna hate it."

"You know I will do anything you ask of me, Boss. What you want me to do?"

"I need you to be Mrs. Black's bodyguard."

"You're right, Boss, me hate that job." Napoleon dropped his head and shook it. "Don't get me wrong, Boss. As I say, I will gladly do anything you ask, and I will lay down me life to protect Mrs. Black. But, Boss, you know Mrs. Black is—let's call it—crafty," He paused and looked at Black, "which make it extremely hard to protect her."

"I know. And that is exactly why I can't trust that job to anybody but you," Black said.

Now all he had to do is convince Shy.

"I think that you need a bodyguard."

Shy's face contorted. "Why?"

"Because I think you need one."

"No I don't. You know I can take care of myself, Michael."

I CAME TO BRING THE PAIN

After the incident with Jada West, Shy was forced to admit that she wasn't a very good shot. She felt like she should have been able to drop all of her attackers that night, without having to call Black for help. *And then put a bullet in that bitches brain.*

In response to that, and without Black's knowledge, Shy had been going to the neighborhood shooting range to practice. After seeing how bad a shot Shy was, one of the women who frequented the range regularly had been giving Shy some pointers, and she was getting better. If she had to have a bodyguard they would tell Black, and that would ruin the surprise. Her intention was to invite Black to the range once she had become a better shot.

"I'm serious, Michael. I do *not* need a bodyguard because I already have one, and I am looking at him. I am absolutely safe with you for protection." Shy smiled and hoped that it would fly, but knew it wouldn't.

"I can't always be there."

"I can take care of myself," Shy insisted.

"Cassandra, please. You've been kidnapped twice, and I am not about to let that happen again. So like it or not, you're getting a bodyguard. So choose one."

"I don't want or need one because I can take care of myself, Michael."

"Okay, gangster. Either you pick somebody or Rain becomes your bodyguard."

"Napoleon. At least I got him trained." It wasn't that she had a problem with Rain. It was just that Rain was already overprotective and obsessive of Black when it came to his safety. Shy could only imagine what she'd be like if Black assigned Rain to protect her.

"Good choice," Black said especially since Napoleon was his choice, too.

That afternoon, Napoleon was reading the New York Carib News when the doorbell rang. He put the paper down, got up and went to answer the door. "What up, Purple Rain?" he said loudly, knowing how much Rain hated it.

"If you don't stop fuckin' calling me that, I'ma fuckin' shoot your West Indian ass in the fuckin' eye," Rain said and handed him a bag.

"Did you bring me some Tabasco?"

"They ain't have no hot sauce, much less Tabasco?" Rain sat down at the table and took out her chicken.

"What you mean, they don't have hot sauce?"

"I'm telling you, Napoleon, bitch looked at me like I had slapped her mama when I asked her for hot sauce."

Napoleon shook his head. "Me starving since M go back to Freeport."

"Shy don't cook at all?"

"I don't think Mrs. Black has been in the kitchen since them move here."

"I heard that," Shy said as she came down the stairs. "And for your information, I have been in the kitchen since we moved here. I haven't touched a pot, but I have been in there."

Shy sat down and looked at the food on the table and looked at Rain. "I know Napoleon hasn't left this house—so, Rain, you went and got food and didn't ask me if I wanted anything?"

"You was sleep. I wasn't about to knock on that door and wake you and Black up after the night we had."

"I can't argue with you about that. But still, I'm hungry," Shy said and thought about the hell of a night they'd had the night before.

The attack came, compliments of Rob Berry. He and his men had been going at them hard since he and Gee Cameron had gotten together and talked after the grand reopening of Cuisine.

"I heard it was you that tried to kill me when you blew up the restaurant," Cameron said.

"Who told you some shit like that?"

"Rain Robinson."

"Rain? You shouldn't believe nothing that murdering psychopath says," Rob Berry said.

"I didn't even know you knew her that well."

"That bitch has been in my ear since Sonny Hill got killed."

"She's been in my ear, too," Cameron admitted reluctantly. He thought that Rain was digging him. The longer the two men talked, the more they realized that the only problem that they had was Rain Robinson.

"We let that bitch play both of us," Rob Berry said.

Now knowing that it was always Rain playing one against the other, they turned against her. The next night, Smoke called and told Rain that he was outside waiting for her.

"I'll be right down."

Rain put on her vest and then her coat; she armed herself and left her apartment. Rain was riding down in the elevator thinking about riding by J.R.'s, and then she would go by Cuisine and check on Black.

When she came out of the building, Rain looked around and saw Smoke standing by the car. As Rain got closer to his car, Smoke saw an old Chevrolet coming at them fast. When he saw the gun come out the window, he started running toward Rain.

"Gun!" Smoke yelled. "Get down!"

As soon as Rain looked and saw the Chevy coming, they opened fire and hit her in the chest. Rain went down. Smoke hit the ground and crawled to Rain. As bullets flew over their heads, Rain and Smoke laid motionless. Once the car had driven on, they both looked up.

"You all right?" Smoke asked.

"Yeah, you?" Rain said. Once again, she was glad she'd worn her vest.

"Yeah, I'm all right." Smoke got up and helped Rain get to her feet. "Wonder who that was?"

"I don't know. Could be Brill and them or fuckin' Rob Berry and Gee Cameron, or it might be the Latin's. But I can guarantee you this: the shit is just beginning, so you better get used to it."

Later that night while Rain was at J.R.'s, her snitch, Dee, came with a message. "What's that?" Smoke asked.

"He said if the bitch is still alive, tell her that Gee Cameron sends his regards."

"And Gee told you that shit personally?" Rain asked.

"Yes."

"You tell that mutha fucka that I'm still alive and I'm gonna cut his dick off and shove it up his ass right before I put two in his brain."

Since that night, Rob Berry and Gee Cameron have made consistent attempts to kill not only Rain, but Black as well. The night before was no different.

It had been quiet for a few days, so Black and Shy decided to have dinner at a nice restaurant downtown. "Not without me," Rain said, and she told Napoleon to take the night off.

They went to Asia Kan on Amsterdam Avenue, which offered a deliciously unique cuisine of Pan Asia fare. Under the stunning white jade Buddha which rested peacefully on top of the sushi bar and beneath the dazzling skylights, they dined on an amazing Thai-style duck appetizer. Then Shy had the red curry salmon and Rain tried the crispy red snapper, while Black chose the char grilled Chilean sea bass.

After dinner, Black excused himself and headed toward the men's room; but he didn't notice that two men followed him. He went into the men's room and stood in one of the stalls, just as the men entered the bathroom. Once they were in the men's room, the men drew their weapons. One stepped up behind Black. As soon as he got close enough, Black turned quickly, grabbed his attacker's hand and punched him in the face. The other man came at him and Black pushed his attacker into him.

There wasn't much room in there to maneuver, so Black had to use that to his advantage. Black grabbed him by his shirt and pulled him to his feet. He reached back and hit him in the face. The other man got to his feet and swung at Black. He stepped to the side and wrapped his arm around his attacker's neck. He struggled to get free, but then Black rammed him face-first into the wall. He went down. The other man came at Black swinging, but he ducked out of the way.

Then Black took out his gun, shot his attacker, and then shot the one on the floor. Black put away his gun and walked out of the men's room. "We need to get out of here," he said when he got back to the table.

"What's wrong?" Shy asked as her and Rain got up.

"I just killed two men in the bathroom."

There was no more discussion necessary. Both Shy and Rain grabbed their coats and Black tossed some money on the table. Rain led the way to the door; but when she opened it, Rain saw three guns pointed at her. Before either Rain or the shooters could do anything, Black came through the door with both guns drawn.

He fired and shot two of the men several times. Shy came out behind Black and quickly got the third man with two shots. "Let's get outta here." Shy put her gun in her purse and walked away.

Black put away his weapons. "Did you recognize them?" he asked as they headed for the car.

"Those are Rob Berry's people," Rain replied.

They were almost to the car when Rain saw four men get out of a car with their weapons drawn. "Get down!" Rain yelled.

The men opened fire with semi-automatic weapons and began firing at them. Black and Shy ducked down behind a car while Rain fired wildly at the men. One of her shots hit its target. He went down and Rain took cover.

Black came up blasting and he hit another man, and his weapons kept firing as he went down. Shy reached in her purse and pulled out her Beretta PX4 Storm. She rose up, took aim, and fired and dropped one of the shooters. Shy took cover as the remaining man began shooting as he ran down the street.

"I got him!" Rain yelled and ran after him.

"Get the car!" Black tossed Shy the keys and ran after Rain.

She ran down the street firing shots as she ran. The man kept firing until he was empty. Rain had made a reputation for herself running men down in heels. When she emptied her clip, Rain reloaded on the run and continued firing.

Meanwhile, Shy had just about made it to the car when she saw an Acura and a Suburban coming at her fast. The Suburban drove by, but the Acura slowed down. When she saw the gun come out the window, Shy dove for the ground. She lay motionless until the car drove on. Shy got to her feet and made it to the car. She got in, started up, and drove away fast.

Rain was fast running in her heels so she was able to close the distance between them. He kept running until he reached the next corner and Rain raised her weapon and fired three shots. He went down.

As soon as Black got there, the Suburban pulled up. Three more men got out and they fired on him and Rain. Once again, they were forced to take cover behind some cars. Rain rose up and shot back as Black reloaded his weapons. He opened fire with both guns and quickly dropped back behind the car. Then he stood up again and hit one with a shot to the head.

Rain leaned over the hood of the car and fired at her target until her guns were empty and he went down. The shooting began again and she took cover.

Just then another car came speeding toward them, and then came screeching to a stop. Shy jumped out of the car and fired on them with the Beretta Px4. Black and Rain stood up and fired at them as they made their way to the car.

"Get in!" Black shouted and kept firing until both Shy and Rain were in the car, before he shot and killed the last two men.

Black got in. "Go," he said, and Shy drove off quickly.

Since Shy was tired from the night before, she decided to stay home and go to bed early. After Rain swept the car, she drove Black to Conversations to talk with Jackie. When they got there, they walked right by FBI Agent Bridgette McCullough.

After the murder of Agent Dawson, McCullough was not convinced that Agent Dawson's death was at the hands of Kevin McCarty. She thought that Black had ordered the hit. Between working with Dawson and the file that she confiscated, she knew all there was to know about Black's organization.

She began hanging out at spots that she knew Black ran every night, identifying all the players on the org chart and adding new ones. From that, McCullough knew that they were at war. She posted up at the bar every night, observing who came and went.

Lola and Kayo's arrival at Conversations didn't go unnoticed by Agent McCullough. "I'm not jealous of her. She does her thing and I do what I do. I just can't stand her."

"Why is that?"

"You just don't know how much of a bitch Cristal is," Lola said as she and Kayo passed McCullough.

It didn't take the agent long to realize that two people were conspicuous by their absence. McCullough had been hanging out in their spots for a month and she hadn't seen Lanisha Henderson. And more importantly, there was no sign of their lawyer, Wanda Moore. There was some word on the street that Wanda was running things from a secure location.

"Yeah, right. Both those bitches are probably dead."

Black and Rain were on their way to the steps that led upstairs when they saw Jackie and Spence seated at a table near the back of Conversations. After Jackie updated Black and Rain on what they needed to know about the war, Black told her that he wanted her to takeover her old game, and informed her that Flip now worked for her.

"Victor says he's a good man, so work with him."

Black thought for a moment that he could use Victor in the war. He liked and trusted Victor and had put him in that spot hoping that Victor would build his own crew. Since that didn't happen, he was good with Victor running the gambling operation that Jada was going to open in the area. It wasn't lost on Black that since they were at war, that Jada was a target, too. Having Victor with her wasn't a waste of a valuable asset.

"You send Sonny back over there and he takes that bunch with him."

"I'm gonna need to recruit some new ho's for that spot," Jackie said.

"You leave that to me." Black understood that he didn't need to waste Jackie's time on recruiting new women, when that was something that Jada West could do—and she did it well.

While Black was meeting with Rain, Spence and Jackie, elsewhere in the club, Leon Copeland's younger sister, Angel, and her friend, Avonte Petrocelli, were at the bar at Conversations. It had been a while since Angel had seen Black. The last time was when Avonte was in trouble.

"What's up, Angel?" Black asked when he got on the phone with Angel that last time.

"I need your help, Mike."

"That's the only time you call me these days, is when you need help."

"Well, you are my other big brother," Angel said, and she gave Black her innocent little-girl giggle. "Who else I'ma call but you? Besides, when my brother left the city, you said you'd look out for me."

That night, Black told Avonte to get whatever she needed from her apartment. Then he told Angel and Avonte to leave and not come back to the apartment until he called Angel. When Black's people were done with the apartment, Avonte never knew what they did with the bodies or how they got all the blood from the carpet or the mattress.

When Angel saw Black sitting there, she told Avonte that she would be back and started for the table. "Mike Black!" she yelled when she got near the table.

Black turned around and saw that it was Angel. Not recognizing her, Rain and Spence pulled their guns. Jackie pulled both of hers. Angel stopped and put up her hands as Agent McCullough looked on.

Black held up one hand. "Everybody relax." He stood up and they all lowered their weapons. Black walked up to Angel and she hugged him. "When you get back in town?"

"'Bout a month ago."

"And this is the first time I'm seeing you? You must be staying out of trouble."

"You make it sound like the only time I call is when I need something."

"I'm just saying," Black said as Avonte came up behind Angel.

"Mike, you remember my friend Avonte, don't you?"

"How could I forget her?" Black looked at Avonte. "How are you, Avonte?"

"I'm doing fine, Mr. Black."

Avonte saw how Angel was looking at Jackie. She'd seen that look on Angel's face many times before. Jackie looked at Angel and then noticed how Avonte was looking at Angel. She laughed to herself.

Black sat down. "Angel, Avonte, that's Rain, Spence and Jackie. Angel is Leon's sister."

"Nice to meet you all," Angel said to everybody, but the only person that she was looking at was Jackie.

"What are you doing tomorrow, Angel?"

"I don't have any plans. What did you have in mind?"

"Why don't you—and Avonte of course, meet me at Cuisine for dinner? I want you to meet my wife."

"Leon said that your wife was dead."

"Guess not, if I'm gonna introduce you to her tomorrow."

"Sounds good, Mike. We'll see you then," Angel said and walked away.

"It was good to see you again, Mr. Black."

"Good to see you, too."

"I never did get a chance to say thank you for what you did for me."

"Don't mention it. To anybody. Ever."

"I won't."

"Avonte!" Angel shouted.

"You better go and see what Angel wants," Black said.

"I'll see you tomorrow," Avonte said and rushed to catch up with Angel.

"I think we need to take this to the office," Rain suggested.

"Agreed." Black got up and everybody headed for the office.

10

Once they were in Jackie's office, Rain wasted no time getting to her point. "I know you said you didn't wanna go on offense against the Latin's, Black," Rain said, "but they've been coming at us pretty hard."

"Recommendations?"

"Since this thing went down, I've had somebody keeping an eye on them. Right now, a man named Hieronimus Balendin is running things. His top people are Terentius Sancho, Ambrosius Faustinus, and his boy, Alano Narez. Since we blew up their warehouse, they've been operating out of a building on Kelly Street. It's a six-story building with an elevator and has thirty-eight apartments and seven stores on the street. Balendin is in an apartment on the top floor."

"Okay, how do we get to him?" Black asked.

"On the side of the building there's an alley. That's how we'll get in."

"Any way of knowing how many men there are in the building?" Black asked.

"Ain't no way to be sure. But there are thirty-eight apartments."

"Which means that there are more than thirty-eight places to hide men."

"That's the problem with goin' in on the ground floor."

"What's that?"

"We might be talkin' 'bout fightin' our way up five floors before we even make it to his."

"I don't like the sound of that," Jackie said.

"Neither do I," Black added. "Think of another way."

Rain took a deep breath. "There are two other ways we can do this. We still go in the alley, but we go up the fire escape. The dark will give us enough cover to get into the building without being seen."

"Or?"

"The building next to it is three floors with a basement, so the roof is just about even with the fifth floor. We go across on a zip line to the fire escape, and then go in on the fifth floor."

"We got the equipment to do that safely?" Spence asked.

"Shit yeah."

"Who's your team?" Black asked.

"Kayo, Treach, Mitch, Ice, and me."

"No, you don't go. Send Spence instead. He'll be in charge," Black said and Spence wasn't liking the idea of going from one building to another on a zip line five stories above the pavement. After the meeting, Rain wanted to know why Black didn't want her to go.

"'Cause you are much too valuable to me to run the risk of losing you. You and me both need to learn to take a step back and let our people do the work."

"I understand."

Later that next night at three in the morning, the team arrived at the building on Kelly Street. Kayo, Treach, Mitch and Ice, along with Spence, went in the building and proceeded to the roof. Once they attached their lines and each men made it safely across to the fifth floor fire escape, they went in.

"Kayo, Treach, you're with me," Spence said.

Mitch looked at his watch. "Give us five minutes before you move," he said, and Ice followed Mitch down the hall.

When they reached the elevator, Ice stood guard while Mitch disabled the elevator. After walking through and checking out the fifth floor, they returned to the staircase to join the rest of the team.

Meanwhile, Spence, Kayo, and Treach made their way up the stairs and were surprised that they didn't encounter any resistance. They got to the sixth floor and waited until they were joined by Mitch and Ice. Once they were set, the team entered the sixth floor.

"Mitch, watch the stairs. Treach, you take that end of the hallway. Ice, Kayo, you're with me," Spence said.

As Treach made his way toward the other end of the hallway, Kayo heard a noise. "Somebody's coming," he said.

Spence moved quickly to the door, while the others took cover. Ice positioned himself on the other side of the door and waited.

One man came out of one of the apartments. Ice grabbed him and covered his mouth. Spence shoved a gun in his face. "¿Dónde está, Balendin?"

"Six-one-three."

"No voy a hacerte daño. ¿Entiendes?"

"Si," the man said and quickly returned to his apartment

At the same time, Mitch saw two men coming up the stairs. He took aim and fired two shots. Two bodies dropped.

Spence went to apartment six-thirteen, picked the lock, opened the door, and then Kayo and Ice followed him inside with their guns pointed. Balendin was asleep alone in the bed. They quietly surrounded the bed and took aim. Balendin began to stir, opened his eyes, and saw the three men surrounding his bed. Then all three men fired.

Kayo looked at Spence. "This was too easy," he said as they left the apartment.

"Let's get out of here," Spence said and led the team down the steps.

They were unaware that the bodies Mitch dropped had been discovered. Once they came out on the fifth floor, men began firing at them. Spence ran for cover in the stairwell with the rest of his team and returned fire as they made it down the steps.

The door to the lobby was open and at first glance, there was no sign of anybody. When Spence peeked around the corner, he saw two men. One was by the front door and another closer to him. The one closest to him was standing by the elevator.

They opened the door and were about to start toward the front door, but were seen. Ice came through the door firing. Mitch picked one off. Treach caught another one with a shot to the chest. Spence shot the man twice as he walked to the door.

"Thanks for your cooperation, gentlemen."

11

It was a little after eight o'clock in the morning and Carmen Taylor had just come in from her five-mile morning run. While she was dining on her usual breakfast of yogurt and coffee, Carmen thought about spending the day shopping. She had talked to Jada West the night before and they had made plans to go shopping that afternoon.

They had talked briefly a few times since Black and Shy had to come to their rescue. She was getting to like Jada. She reminded Carmen of some of the models she used to hang out with in Europe. Despite that, there was a part of Carmen that wondered if there was a hidden agenda behind Jada continuing to reach out to her. Other than Black, the one thing that they had in common was that they were both clothes horses. Both Carmen and Jada were passionate about the clothes they wore.

After she finished eating, Carmen went into the room in her apartment that she converted into a clothes closet and thought about what she was going to wear. Normally, she would just throw on some pencil leg jeans and some pumps, but she was shopping with Jada West that day.

"What do you wear when you go shopping with Jada West?" Carmen asked herself and then she laughed. "It's not a competition."

But Carmen understood perfectly that on some level it was, and she was determined not to be out dressed by Jada. With that central thought in mind, Carmen selected an A.L.C. Bechet leather dress and Manolo Blahnik BB suede point-toe pumps.

I CAME TO BRING THE PAIN

When Carmen arrived at the Kimberly Hotel, she was about to call up to Jada's room to let her know she was there and then she would make herself comfortable and wait for Jada to make a Jada West entrance.

"Good morning, Carmen," Jada said.

Carmen turned around quickly and was shocked to see Jada and Victor standing there. Despite the fact that Jada was wearing a floor-length leather coat with a fur collar, Carmen could see what she had on. Jada wore a Carolina Herrera floral stripe dress and Alejandro Ingelmo Mariposa, leather tie-up pumps.

"Hey, Jada. I love those shoes."

"Thank you, Carmen. They're Alejandro Ingelmo," Jada said and Carmen knew that they must have cost her at least a thousand dollars.

"Hey, Victor."

"Good morning, Ms. Taylor," Victor said.

"You really do need to start calling me Carmen."

Jada giggled. "He can't."

"He can't?"

"No, Carmen, he can't."

"Why?"

"Tell her why, Victor," Jada said, and Carmen could tell just how much Jada was enjoying this.

"Mr. Black said to treat you ladies with respect at all times. So you are Ms. Taylor and she is Ms. West." Victor paused and pointed back and forth between the two of them. "Not Carmen, and never Jada," he said as Jada tipped her head to one side, batted her eyes and laughed a little.

"You just gotta love that man," Carmen said.

Victor extended his arm graciously. "Shall we go ladies?"

"Of course," Jada said and she and Carmen walked toward the front door with Victor following behind them.

Carmen leaned closer to Jada. "Victor is so cute."

"Isn't he," Jada said.

"Must be nice to have a cutie follow you around all day."

"Carmen, please. Mr. Black is at war. I know you're not foolish enough to think for one single second that one of these sexy black men around here isn't following you around all day."

Carmen thought about it and knew Jada was right. "You just gotta love that man."

Since Jada hadn't eaten they grabbed a bite, and then they got to shopping with a vengeance. Both Carmen and Jada had boutiques that they liked to shop at. By late afternoon, they had been to Chloe New York on Madison Avenue, D Porthault on Park, Smith on Sullivan, which was conveniently located on Sullivan Street, and agnès b New York on Greene Street. Their next stop was EMc2 on Elizabeth, but first they went to Otte on Third Avenue.

Jada was looking at an abstracted, Akris Stable San Cristobal print silk dress. It was a uniquely colorful boat neck, sleeveless, with a concealed side zip print, which was impeccably tailored from imported Italian silk. As she looked at the dress, Jada wondered, as she always did, how Black would like her in the dress. Jada slowly drifted into memories of what happened that night after she left the key card for him.

Black knocked on the door and shortly thereafter, Jada opened the door dressed in a red sleeveless La Perla gown, highlighted by dramatic lace insets, and a scoop neckline with a keyhole back that clung to every inch of her body.

"Evening, Mr. Black."

"Hello, Ms. West."

Black looked at Jada and began thinking that this was definitely a bad idea. He had an overwhelming urge to bend Jada over the nearest piece of furniture and fuck the shit out of her, because she was looking sexy as hell, and he knew just how good that pussy would feel.

"Won't you come in?" Jada smiled and was about to step aside when something happened that she wasn't expecting.

"No, Ms. West, I won't." Black reached in his pocket and came out with the room card key that Jada had laid on the table earlier that evening.

"I just came to give this back to you." Black handed the card key to Jada. "And to tell you that once you conclude your business in the city, you need to go back to Nassau before Mrs. Black kills you. And believe me, Mrs. Black *will* kill you."

"I see." He could see the look of pain, hurt and disappointment wash across Jada's face.

"Good night, Ms. West."

"Good night, Mr. Black."

Black smiled. "We'll talk again soon. And this time, I actually will talk to you soon." Black turned and walked away.

Jada watched him walk down the hall, then she closed the door and for the first time since Vivian wrote her from jail and told her not to write or visit, Jada West sat down and cried.

Once she had gotten it out of her system, Jada got up, fixed herself a drink, and began plotting her next move. Despite what Shy had said and her warning—and Jada took that warning very seriously—Mike Black was her man, too. And Jada was determined to have her share of her man back.

"Jada!" Carmen shouted to bring Jada out of her trance.

Jada looked at Carmen and smiled. "Excuse me?"

"Where were you?"

"I beg your pardon?"

"You've been standing there for the last five minutes staring at that Akris print."

"Was I really?"

"Yes, Jada, you were. Where were you?" Carmen asked, and then she thought about it. "Never mind. I know exactly where you were." Carmen took the dress from Jada. "Come on."

"Where are we going?"

"We need to talk."

"As long as it involves cocktails," Jada said, and they caught a cab to Sofia Wine Bar on East 50th Street.

12

Redbrick walls, shelves of gleaming wine bottles, and a dark wooden bar give the small Sofia Wine Bar a simple, relaxed feel. The café is lit by chandeliers, large quartz candle holders, and tin lanterns, where waiters drifted between the tables helping customers choose from over ninety wines that were served by the glass. But Carmen and Jada were not there to sample the wine.

While Victor took a seat at the bar, Carmen and Jada were shown to a table. "What can I get you, ladies?"

"The lady will have a French 75."

"With Rémy Martin XO," Jada said quickly.

"And for you?"

"I'll have a shot of Ron Zacapa XO on the rocks. Some spinach dip, and—," she looked at Jada. "And bring my frowned up friend over there the cheese platter."

The waiter left and Jada looked at Carmen. "Do I look that bad?"

"Like somebody stole your joy."

"Somebody did."

Carmen laughed. "Yeah, and her name is Cassandra Black."

"Ha, ha, ha—fuck you, Carmen Taylor."

"Have you noticed that since you spent that night with her shooting up everything in sight, that you have developed quite the potty mouth. Before that night, you were always so ladylike."

"I say again, fuck you, Carmen Taylor," Jada said, this time she gave her the finger to go along with it and then she laughed. "Well she did. I was a happy woman until she came back from the dead."

"The nerve of her."

"I mean really, Carmen, who does that? Most dead people have the decency to stay dead and not show up five or whatever years later and ruin people's lives," Jada said as the waiter returned with their drinks.

"I'll be back with your food in a few," the waiter said and turned to leave.

"Excuse me?"

The waiter turned back to Jada. "Yes, ma'am?"

"Would you bring me another, please," Jada said.

"You haven't touched that one yet."

"I will by the time you get back. Now run along." Jada motioned.

"That was a French 75."

"With Rémy Martin XO, please."

"Right away."

After the waiter left, Carmen glanced at Jada and shook her head. "Mike must have changed his drink."

Jada picked up her glass and sipped her drink. "You think you're so smart, don't you; Carmen Taylor? Maybe I'm drinking XO because you're drinking XO."

Carmen laughed. "That was so weak it isn't even funny."

"I know, wasn't it?" They both laughed.

"You see how that man got you, Jada?"

"Yes, and its pitiful."

"You gotta let him go and move on."

Jada looked at Carmen. "Like you did?"

They looked at each other for a second or two.

"I'm sorry, Carmen. That was mean and it was beneath me."

"Yes, Jada, it was. It was both mean and beneath you, but you're right. Maybe I haven't let go, but I have moved on." The waiter returned with Jada's drink. "When you bring the food, you can bring me another."

"That was Ron Zacapa XO, correct?"

Carmen nodded her head and then she looked at Jada. "I was just like you once: hanging around, doing things to try and get him to acknowledge that I was alive." Carmen laughed. "At least you've got to see him a couple of times. Back then, Bobby and Freeze wouldn't let me get anywhere near him."

"What did you do to get to the point where you could move on?"

"I worked. I threw myself into my career."

Jada took a sip of her drink. "Can I ask you a personal question?"

"Go ahead."

"Not that I'm trying to make this a competition," Jada began, but she understood as Carmen did, that it clearly was. "But I'm interested to know what happened between you and Mr. Black?" Jada paused and Carmen just looked at her. "I mean, he left me to go back to his wife. Why did he leave you?"

Carmen looked at Jada. "You remember that I said that it was because of Mike that I became a model?"

"Yes. You said that he introduced you to your agent and he made you take your career seriously."

"What I didn't say was that all that happened because Calvin, that's my agent, went to see Mike and told him that he thought I could be great."

"He was certainly right about that."

"He was. And I was blowing it, because back then—all I wanted to be was Mike's woman. Then Calvin told Mike that for my sake, he should let me go so I could become somebody. He broke up with me that same night. I didn't see Mike again for years after that."

"You just gotta love that man," Jada said quietly.

The waiter arrived, placed Carmen's drink in front of her and served the food. "And I took the liberty of bringing you another French 75."

"Thank you. Somebody must have mentioned that I'm an excellent tipper," Jada said.

"Will there be anything else, ladies?"

"I think we can manage for a minute. But don't wait too long before you come back and check on us."

While Jada talked to the waiter, Carmen looked at the bar and noticed that there was a man sitting and talking to Victor, but she couldn't see his face. Carmen picked up her drink and wondered if the man was the bodyguard that Jada suggested Black had assigned to her. She smiled, and then Carmen looked at Jada as the waiter walked away. "I was nineteen. And my ambition in life was to have a bunch of his babies." Carmen laughed.

"What's funny?" Jada asked.

"When I finally did see Mike again, we had a chance to talk about it."

"How did it happen that you got to see him again?"

I CAME TO BRING THE PAIN

"I was dating a lawyer named Marcus Douglas, and one night we had dinner with an old friend of his from law school. That turned out to be Wanda."

"I hate her."

"I never liked Wanda, either. She could be such a bitch when she wanted to be," Carmen said.

Jada rolled her eyes in complete agreement. "Tell me about it."

"Anyway, later that night I went to see Mike at Cuisine and I asked him if he remembered the last thing he said to me, and he sort of remembered."

"What did he say?"

"He said that I would be better off without a thug nigga like him in my life. And he actually did say that. But it wasn't the last thing he said."

"Well, what was the last thing he said?"

"I was sitting there, on the brink of tears, and he said, 'I'm going to the store. You want anything?'"

"That's it?"

"That's it."

"And you said?"

"Bring me back a Diet Pepsi." Carmen smiled. "That next night when I got off work, Mike was standing outside the door waiting for me with a Diet Pepsi."

"You just gotta love that man," Jada said.

"And maybe that's one reason why I still do. But my point is that I moved on and someday, if you're lucky, you'll get over him or you'll find somebody."

"But you never have; have you, Carmen?"

"No, Jada, I haven't. Not really."

"What about the lawyer you were dating?"

"As much as we tried, Marcus and I just couldn't get it to work."

"Mr. Black is a difficult act to follow."

"Tell me about it." Carmen raised her glass and Jada thought for a second.

Going after Mr. Black this way is definitely not the move for me. The thing to do is to go back to Nassau as they have insisted. Once I conclude my business, of course. The next time Mr. Black sees me, I will be what he once saw in me: a superior business woman with a touch of class and the ability to make him piles of money. I will be looking sensational, and I will make him regret the day that he let a woman like me get away.

Jada laughed to herself.

I'll make Mr. Black want me. That's the way to get him back. Not running around here like a defenseless school girl.

Jada raised her glass and she drank to that.

13

The following afternoon, Black and Bobby were having lunch at Cuisine. Black had the Shrimp Creole while Bobby enjoyed the Mango Chicken. Over lunch and drinks, Black explained to Bobby that he had Rain go on offense the night before against Benitez's people. He was just about to tell Bobby about his long-term plan for dealing with them, when Rain came in and joined them at the table.

"What's up, Rain?"

"What's up, y'all?"

"How'd it go last night?" Black asked.

"Other than Spence swearing that he'll never get on a fuckin' zip line again, it went fine."

When Phillip, the head waiter, saw Rain come in Cuisine, he quickly rushed to the bar, got her a drink, and then he placed a shot of Patrón in front of Rain. "Can I bring you anything, Ms. Robinson?" he asked.

"I ain't too hungry, Phillip, so just bring me a crab cake burger," Rain said.

"Right away, Ms. Robinson. Can I get anything else for you gentlemen?"

"You can take this plate and bring me another shot of Rémy," Bobby said.

"What about you, Mr. Black; can I take your plate and bring you another drink?"

"Go ahead. Thank you, Phillip."

Once Phillip cleared the table, Black looked at Rain. "I'm glad you're here. I was just about to explain to Bobby exactly how I plan on dealing with Benitez's crowd going forward," he said and laid it out for them.

59

"You think he'll go for it?" Bobby asked.

"I think so. One, because he owes me a favor and two, because it's too much money for him to pass on."

"That will take a lotta heat off me," Rain said. "When you gonna make that happen?"

"That's the problem. My people down there tell me that he is out of the country and won't be back for at least another week."

"Any idea where he is?"

"No, all of his people are very close mouthed about where he went or exactly when he'll be back. I just gotta wait to hear from them."

"Let's hope it happens soon. Them Latin's are getting more aggressive," Rain said as Phillip returned to the table with food and drinks.

"You keep your foot on their necks then, Rain. At this point, it can only strengthen our position when I go to make this deal."

"You know what's funny?" Bobby asked.

"What's that, Bob?"

"We've been bullets flying for weeks and we haven't seen Kirk walk through that door."

"As a matter of fact, he hasn't, and that is unusual for the detective."

"Ain't y'all heard?" Rain asked and took a bite of her crab cake burger. "Kirk's on suspension pending investigation by Internal Affairs."

"For what?"

"I don't know all the details, but the way I get it, Kirk killed two niggas after they shot him and his partner."

Bobby laughed. "I'd kill some niggas to over shooting that sexy ass mutha fucka he got for a partner," he said, and both Bobby and Rain laughed.

But not Black.

Not only did he like and respect the detective for being the kind of man he was, but he owed Kirk his freedom.

When Black was arrested and accused of murdering Shy, it was Kirk that went out of his way to prove that Black could not have committed the crime. For that, Black was grateful and he swore that someday, somehow he would pay the detective back.

"See if you can't find out exactly what's going on with Kirk," Black ordered.

14

For Detective Kirkland this was a strange time. His troubles began the morning after he tracked down and murdered Donaldo Baker and his cousin, Aston Simpson. That morning at the Baker crime scene, Lieutenant Sanchez was wondering why he'd been called there. That is, until he was told who the victim was.

As soon as Sanchez heard that, he knew that Kirk had tricked him and killed Baker. In that split second, he realized that Kirk knew he was going to kill Baker and didn't want him to have any part in it. Sanchez was about to get out of there and had just turned to leave, when he saw Captain Keys coming his way. Fast.

"I need to talk to you, Lieutenant," Keys said as he approached.

"Que pasa, Captain?"

"What do you know about this?"

"It's a dead body," Sanchez said somewhat sheepishly.

"I know it's a fuckin' dead body, Lieutenant. But it's the same guy that Kirk said shot him and Bautista."

"Is it?"

"Don't play games with me, Sanchez. You know that's who it is, so let's stop fucking around. You were seen leaving the hospital with Kirk and a few hours later, this asshole gets murdered. Now what do you have to say about that?"

"When I left the hospital with Kirk, I took him home. He was groggy from the pain meds he's on, so he went to bed."

"So, for the record, you have no knowledge of this and weren't with Kirk last night."

"You think Kirk smoked this guy?"

Before the captain could answer, Detective Hunter, who was assigned to the case, walked by.

"If this is the fuck that shot Kirk and Bautista—I'm saying, if this is the fuck that shot two cops, then I say fuck him all the way to hell. And if Kirk did kill this bastard, all I can say is that I'm sorry I wasn't with him so I could've shot the bastard, too."

The detective walked away before the captain could say anything. In the weeks that followed, the captain found that would be the attitude of most, if not all of the officers in his command.

But that day, he was still pushing it and pushing it hard. "Come on," Keys told Sanchez.

"Where are we going?"

"To see the other bastard Kirk killed last night."

When Keys and Sanchez were finished viewing the Aston Simpson crime scene, the captain was more convinced than ever that Kirk was responsible for both murders.

"According to the timeline that's developing, after Kirk left the hospital and ditched you, he came here first. He made this guy tell him where Baker was and then he killed him."

"What makes you so sure that Kirk did this?" Sanchez asked, even though he was convinced too.

Keys got in the lieutenant's face. "Because I don't believe in coincidences. Kirk killed both of them."

"Don't you think you should wait to see where the investigation leads before you come to that kind of conclusion? I mean, this is America, you know; a man is innocent until proven guilty."

"That's bullshit and you know it, Sanchez," Keys said as he parked near Kirk's apartment. "Come on, Lieutenant. Let's go have a talk with your innocent man."

Keys and Sanchez got out of the car, walked to Kirk's apartment and knocked on the door. When there was no answer, Sanchez got the spare key that Kirk had duck taped to the welcome mat and let them in.

"Kirk!" Sanchez shouted. "You here?"

"Probably on the run," Keys said as Sanchez wandered around.

"Captain, he's right here."

Keys walked to where Sanchez was standing and saw Kirk in bed with a bottle of pills on the bed next to him.

"Kirk!" Keys shouted, but Kirk didn't move.

Sanchez moved closer to the bed and shook him. "Kirk."

After a while, Kirk began to stir. He looked at Sanchez and then he saw Keys. "What are you guys doing in my apartment?"

"You didn't answer the door," Keys said, and Sanchez cut him off.

"The captain's got this wild idea that you killed two people last night."

Kirk laughed and sat up in bed. "Who did I kill?"

"Donaldo Baker and Aston Simpson," Keys barked.

"In my dreams."

"So you're telling me that you didn't kill them?"

"You're serious," Kirk said and looked long and hard at both men. "You here to arrest me?"

"No, Kirk, not yet."

"If you're not here to arrest me then get the fuck outta here," Kirk said, laid back down and closed his eyes.

"I think we should respect the man's wishes and leave," Sanchez suggested.

"You can stay as long as you like, Gene. But the guy that just accused me of double homicide, he has to get the fuck outta my apartment," Kirk said without opening his eyes. "Escort him out, Gene."

"Captain." Sanchez extended a gracious hand toward the door.

"I'll go, but if I find out that you did this or had any involvement in it, I'll personally see that you go down for it," Keys said and left the apartment, slamming the door behind him.

Once he was gone, Sanchez sat down in the chair next to the bed. "So, now that he's gone, tell me, did you kill them?"

Kirk just looked at Sanchez and said nothing.

Over the next few weeks, Detective Hunter's investigation into the two murders went nowhere. There was no physical evidence at either crime scene and there were no witnesses. Until all that changed.

Enter Greg Milson, a small-time thief and drug addict. He was arrested on a drug possession charge. After he was processed, Milson told the officer that he had something to trade.

"Something big. But I'll only talk to Internal Affairs."

It took a few days and a lot more requests, but Milson got want he wanted.

"I'm Detective Rodgers." He showed his badge. "Internal Affairs. I understand you have something for me."

"I do, but I walk on the drug charge and you gotta protect me."

"What you got?"

"I saw a detective kill somebody," Milson said and told the detective that he was at the Eden Motel on Boston Road one night, when he saw a detective knock on a door and shoot the man that answered.

"You know the detective's name?"

"Kirk."

Now that he was on suspension, Kirk had spent most of his time at the hospital with Bautista. It was discovered that due to loss of blood flow, there was some evidence of brain injury. Her doctors medically induced a coma to halt blood flow entirely and give the brain time to heal.

Now all Kirk could do was wait for his day in court, sitting at Bautista's bedside. He was still a cop, but at the same time, he really wasn't.

No badge, no gun, no cop.

15

Once she finished her crab cake burger, Rain told Black and Bobby what her next move would be in the war with Gee Cameron and Rob Berry. When she was done, Black approved her plans and made some observations that he was sure would improve what she had in mind. Rain stood up. "I'll make that happen," she said and walked away from the table.

Bobby looked at Rain as she walked away and then to Black. "Is it me or is Rain getting fine on us? I mean, she always had that body, but is she getting better looking?"

"Our little girl is growing up and her looks are maturing."

"She starting to look more like her mama than her ugly ass daddy," Bobby said.

When Rain opened the door to leave Cuisine, Monika walked up. "Hey, Rain," Monika said and gave her a hug.

"When did you get back?" Rain asked, and knew that if Monika was back then Nick was, too.

"This morning, and I came right here."

"Black and Bobby are inside and I know they'll be glad to see you," Rain said and then she left.

Monika went in Cuisine and approached the table where Black and Bobby were seated.

"There she is," Black said.

"Hey, Black. Hey, Bobby."

"Have a seat," Black said. "It's damn sure good to see you."

"So, what's going on?" Black took his time and explained to Monika the results of Wanda's disastrous reign as boss of the family. "That's fucked up," she said.

"Tell me about it," Bobby said.

"There's something's that I could really use you and Nick on." Black paused. "Where is Nick?"

Monika hesitated before responding. "Nick had something that he needed to take care of."

Black looked long and hard at Monika. He didn't like the tone of her voice and knew that something was up. "You wanna tell me about it?"

"Not really. I think it would be best if Nick told you about this himself."

"Okay, tell me anyway."

Monika smiled. "Nick is the father of a sixteen-year-old boy."

"What?" Black said with a shocked look on his face.

"You're kidding, right?" Bobby asked and laughed.

"Nope, not kidding."

"Who's the mother?" Black wanted to know.

"April."

"Dancer?"

"Yup."

"That explains a lot," Black said.

"It does, doesn't it?" Monika laughed. "There was a running joke around the office that Nick and April needed to just fuck and get it over with."

"Who knew they already had," Bobby joked.

"Whenever he gets finished doing whatever it is that he has to do, I got work for you and Nick," Black said.

I CAME TO BRING THE PAIN

Nick's first stop once he returned from Yemen was to see April. After Nick told her that he had confirmation that Marvin was his son, April had the unenviable task of telling her husband that he was not the father. As April had thought, her husband Marvin had suspected for years that he wasn't the boy's biological father. "You found his real father?"

"Yes," April said and then, for the first time in their relationship, she told him the truth and explained the entire situation to Marvin. Once she was done and Marvin was finished asking questions, April asked the next logical question. "What do we do now?"

Marvin paused and contemplated his answer carefully before speaking. "I think that we need to go and have a talk with our son."

At first, it wasn't easy for Marvin Jr. to hear that the man that was standing before him, the man he called daddy, was not actually his father. "But you both lied to me," the young man said. "And don't tell me it was for my own good."

What was just as hard, was for April to tell him the truth of what happened. Marvin saw that she was struggling and stepped in. "What your mother is trying to say is that regardless of everything that's happened, we love you and we always will."

When Nick returned from Sana'a, April introduced Nick to her husband over lunch. She thought that it was important for the two men to meet. Then, later that evening, the three of them spoke to Marvin together. "This is Nick Simmons. He is your biological father," the older

Marvin said. After a while, April left the room and the three men talked.

When he saw that things were going well and that father and son were getting comfortable with each other, Marvin excused himself and left them alone to talk. He went in the other room and sat next to April. She took his hand in hers.

"I want to say thank you for everything you've done to make this easier for everybody," April said.

"What were you expecting me to do, April? Turn my back on everything and just run out? Come on. You know me better than that."

"I didn't know what to expect. You can be very cold and distant sometimes."

"Not when it comes to our—" he paused. "Our son. I have always done what's best for him in the past and I will continue to do what's best for him in the future." Marvin let go of April's hand. "You, April, are another matter."

16

The following day when Nick got to the office, April was locked in her office. After trying to give her the space that she needed, that afternoon, Nick knocked on the door.

"Can I come in?"

April nodded her head and motioned for Nick to come in. As Nick closed the door behind him, April tried her best to conceal the fact that she'd been crying.

"How'd it go last night after I left?" Once he was in her office, it was obvious to Nick that April had been crying.

"Marvin said that he was moving out and then he was going to file for divorce." A lone tear ran down April's cheek and she wiped it away quickly.

"I'm sorry to hear that, April," Nick said, but he knew that on some level that he wasn't sorry to hear it. He felt for April's pain, but at the same time he knew that he was glad to hear that April would soon be a single woman.

Nick stood up. "Go and get your coat."

"Where are we going?"

"Out of here. Now come on," Nick said, and they ended up at Bar Boulud on Broadway.

Since April wasn't very hungry, she ordered the Crevettes Cocktail, which was iceberg lettuce, ruby red shrimp and French cocktail sauce, and then she picked over it. While Nick, who was starving from not eating since he'd left Yemen, had the Quenelle De Brochet. A northern pike quenelle, roasted half lobster, served with burgundy black truffle rice and nantua sauce.

"It's not so much the fact that he's leaving that's bothering me. I've known that our marriage was over for years. We both did. The only thing that was keeping us together was Marvin." April let out a little laugh. "Marvin and the lie. That's what hurt."

"What's that?"

"It was the things that he said about me. What's worse is that what he was saying was the truth. I cheated on him; got pregnant by a man I just met. Then I married him and lied to him for all these years." April stabbed a shrimp and Nick watched breathlessly as it passed her lips. "He said that I should have told him the minute that I knew he wasn't the father. Said I should have given him the choice."

"And he's right, you know?"

"I know, but I thought I was doing what was right at the time. And before you say it, I know I was wrong. It was selfish."

April refused to look up from her plate.

"Hey."

When she still refused to look up, Nick used his finger and tilted her chin up.

"You are not selfish; you just didn't see it all the way through. You, April, are way too caring to be selfish."

For a moment they just looked at each other.

"That's nice of you to say, Nick, but I've made a mess of things."

"How?"

"Marvin can't stand to look at me, and my own son looks at me sideways." April stabbed another shrimp and put it in her mouth. "But I guess that too is to be expected."

During the remainder of the meal, April told Nick about his son. She told him that Marvin was idealistic, enthusiastic, and curious. "And he has a very strong will," April said. "Just like somebody else I know."

Nick smiled a little at April. "You mean his father."

"Yes, Nick, his father."

April got lost in Nick's eyes while she told him, "Marvin will only give in to parental authority if he's convinced there is logic and truth behind what you're saying. Otherwise, he'll continue to ask questions. If you're fair and honest he'll learn to respect you. For the most part, Marvin is a good boy."

"Young man."

"Whatever, Nick. Young man or not, he will always be my little boy," April said, and then thought about what she had said. Nick would never know his son the way that she did; never know him as a little boy. Because of her, Nick had missed his son's first steps, his first words, his first time riding a bike and his first day of school. Her lie had denied Nick all of that.

"I know you must hate me for keeping your son away from you."

"Not necessarily. Things I was doing at that time made me the last person your son—I mean our son— should have been around. No, April, the right man raised him. It seems to me that you and Marvin did an excellent job."

"Thank you for saying that, Nick."

"Now the question is; what about you and I?" Nick asked.

April looked at Nick for a while. "I don't know, Nick. There were times when I thought that I knew exactly what I wanted."

"And now?"

"Honestly, I just don't know." April leaned forward and Nick took her hands in his. "I do know that I find you as physically attractive a man as I did all those years ago. More so now I think, because now I actually know you. Now that I know you, know the kind of man that you are, I find you even more attractive, Nick. You're a man that I've come to admire and respect. When I look at you, I see myself. I see the person that I always wanted to be and always talked myself out of being." April laughed and smiled. "I have no idea how you talked me out of my clothes. Even if I wanted to have sex with you that night, I'm sure I would have talked myself out of it."

"I'm more persuasive than you think I am."

"I know exactly how persuasive you can be, Nick. That's not the issue."

"What's the issue, April?"

"How do you know we are compatible?" April asked.

Nick laughed. "You are inside my head, April, and I'm in yours. We finish each other's sentences. How much more compatible do you want us to be."

"That's exactly my point, Nick. Why should we run the risk of ruining things?"

"I think it will do nothing but enhance what we already have and make it better. Make us better; stronger."

"I disagree, Nick." April shook her head. "It's all a mess and you know that I don't like messes. I like things neat, clean and organized."

"So do I."

"Yeah, after I clean it up for you."

"However *we* get there, *we* get there. And the operative word in that sentence is *we*. We, April, you and I are great together. We're a team."

"A team where you give the orders and I follow them."

Nick smiled. "Whatever works. You can't tell me that we don't work and work well."

"I don't know, Nick," April said softly and sat back, looking unconvinced by anything she was saying. "Whatever happens between us, let's promise to take our time so we don't lose what we already have."

"I promise."

After Nick dropped April off at her house and the two said good night for the evening, he knew that there was something that he needed to do. He had thought about calling and telling her. But Nick knew that this was a conversation that he wanted to have in person.

When he got there, Nick got out of the car and walked down the street to her house. He was surprised that if things were bad enough for Black to want him and Monika home, that there was no security on the block. Nick walked up to the door and rang the bell. When nobody answered, he took out his key and let himself in. Once Nick turned off the alarm and turned on the lights, he saw that all of the furniture had been covered with sheets. Nick looked around the house and found the same thing in each room.

Nick went back in the living room and pulled the sheet off the bar and fixed himself a drink. He drained the glass, poured another, and wondered.

"Where's Wanda?"

17

It has never been easy for Ryder Baker. She would never forget the morning when she returned to the room and found her husband, Donaldo, dead. Every time she closed her eyes, Ryder could see herself standing there looking at his body and crying. Then she pulled herself together enough to pack up all of her stuff, and wipe down the room for fingerprints. Ryder remembered taking one last look at her husband before she closed the door on that part of her life. Since then, Ryder had changed her last name back to Bell, and moved in with her cousin, Mileena Hayes.

Ryder had begun thinking about what she wanted to do with the rest of her life. "Get a minimum wage job and struggle? Not."

"I could get you a job at Impressions waiting tables," Mileena said. She worked there as a bartender.

"Baby girl, I love you. But the next time you say some shit about me, on these feet, hustling drinks for a dollar," Ryder reached in her purse and took out her gun. "I will shoot you in your big ass head."

"You won't kill me."

"What makes you think I won't?"

"'Cause I will tell my mommy on you; and you know your Aunt Lucy don't mind beating your ass." Mileena laughed.

"What you need to do is get me in with that sexy ass Mike Black." On the night her husband was killed, Ryder met Black at Impressions.

"Here are the facts," Mileena said turning serious. "One, Mike Black is the boss, cuz. So maybe you should aim lower. Two, he is married and his wife, Shy, will kill you about that man," Mileena told her. "Besides, they are at war and Black don't have time for you."

With that in mind, Mileena told Jab about Ryder. He wasn't in the muscle side of the family. Jab worked for Howard, who Rain had put in charge of the money making side of the family. Jab was a money maker. Ryder was determined to not only prove herself useful, but that she could earn money as well. The next time both Ryder and Jab were at Impressions, Mileena introduced them.

"Mileena tells me you got skills that I may be able to take advantage of."

Ryder smiled. "I can do anything you need me to do. But I'm good with locks and alarm systems, and what I'm best at is planning the job."

Jab laughed. "Why is that?"

"Because I can anticipate and plan for everything that might go wrong." Ryder paused. "Oh yeah, I'm good with a gun, too."

Once Ryder explained her skills, Jab put her onto something to see what she could do.

"There is a fur warehouse, and I want you to plan the robbery."

Ryder laughed a little. "That's what I do."

The first thing that Ryder did was to go and get herself a new outfit. She bought a blue Escada scuba ruffle front jacket and skirt, a silk ruffle top, with Jimmy Choo pumps and a briefcase. All of which Ryder planned to return the moment she was finished with them.

Now that she was dressed for business, Ryder went to check out the warehouse. She told the manager that she a buyer from Los Angeles who was looking to change suppliers. Ryder even went as far as to dig around in her briefcase like she had business cards that she just couldn't find.

Since she was a pretty woman and had more game than Toys R Us, Ryder was able to convince the manager to take her into the warehouse. While she was back there, he showed her where everything was. She had a photographic memory, so Ryder didn't need to be back there for very long before she had the layout of the place. From that, Ryder formed a plan.

She drew a map of the warehouse for Jab that showed where the exits and cameras were. "I also identified where the expensive pieces are and where the cheap shit is," Ryder said and pointed them out on the map. "That's gonna save you a lot of time, because now you can just walk around and tell them which pieces to get."

The way Ryder planned it out, it was a five man job. "One at the security shack at the gate; another standing guard at the door. Two men to get the stuff, and you, running the show. Piece of cake."

Jab looked at the diagram Ryder had provided and the plan she'd laid out and shook his head. "This is good work."

"Thank you, Jab. When do we do the job?"

"You're not going."

"Why not?"

"You'll get your cut for planning the job, but I have no idea how you respond under pressure."

Ryder looked Jab up and down and wondered if he had what it takes to put her under pressure. Most men didn't. "This is bullshit. I should be there to see it through. But you know what; I'm cool. Let me know how it goes," Ryder said and walked out of the room.

It was a week later, and Ryder was sitting in her usual spot at the bar with Mileena when Jab walked up. "What's up, Ryder," Jab said.

"I'm doin' great."

Jab sat down next to her and handed her an envelope. Ryder put the envelope in her purse and then she picked up her drink.

"How'd it go?"

"We had some problems," Jab said and told Ryder about the things that went wrong. "But we managed to get it done."

Ryder took a sip of her drink. "That's why you should have let me come with you. You know I had plans for all that."

"Yeah, I thought about that."

18

After that, Ryder was in, and she began making a name for herself. Just about every job Jab ran, it was Ryder who planned it out and was there when it was going down.

"What's our next job?" Ryder asked.

"Our next job is going to be the taking of the National Bank and Trust," Jab said, "and I want you to plan it and be part of the team that runs the job. You up for that?"

"I can handle that."

After she cased the bank they were going to hit, Ryder met Jab at the cleaners that Howard runs. "What you got for me today, Ms. Ryder?"

She laid a diagram of the bank and of the area around it on the table. "This branch always has a large amount of cash on hand," Jab began. "And we gonna take it."

He looked at Ryder. "When the bank opens there's always a rush, which ends around ten. We go at ten thirty." Ryder pointed to the diagram of the bank. "The security is stationed just inside of the bank. Slick will be positioned here by the door and Jab will disarm him while I cover. The bank got six people working there. There are four teller positions and three offices across from them. When we hit, at least two, or maybe three of those positions will be manned, but all positions will be stocked with cash. When we go in, I will cover the room."

"We in and out in three minutes and not a second more," Jab said.

"When we get inside, we move everybody to the center of the room. Slick, you clear these offices while Jab moves everybody out from behind the counter. The bank manager will have a key around his neck. Slick takes it from him. After you get the key to the money drawers, you go behind the counter with Jab and get the money in the drawers and from the rolling cart, which will be behind the counter. Take the cart first, Slick, while Jab clears the teller positions."

On the day of the job, each member of the team was dressed in a grey jumpsuit. Jab and Slick assumed a position in front of the National Bank and Trust. Jab and Ryder exited the vehicle and saw the security guard. He watched him until he entered the bank.

Slick got out of the car and moved into position to intercept the security guard, while Ryder held a gun to his head. Slick quickly disarmed the guard and Ryder went inside the bank. "Nobody move!" Ryder yelled.

Slick moved to get the employees out of the offices and took the key from the branch manager. Jab moved everybody out from behind the counter. Soon everybody was in the middle of the room, face down on the floor, and Ryder had them covered.

Everything was working out just as Ryder had planned it. Jab went to each teller's position and cleaned out the drawers, while Slick unlocked the cart and got the money. Jab handed the bag to Slick and moved toward the door to make their escape.

Jab took off his mask and made it to the car and was about to move the car into position when he saw a police car coming toward the bank. Jab wasn't worried, because Ryder had planned for this contingency.

Slick came from behind the counter and handed the bags to Ryder. She took the money and moved toward the door. Slick opened fire with the pump before the cops could get out of their car. Jab got out and he covered Ryder's exit from the bank. Once Ryder had placed the money in the car, she began firing at the police car.

Jab got back in the car while Slick kept firing. Ryder took aim and shot out the rear tires on the police car, and then she got in the car. Once Slick was in the vehicle, Jab took off.

While Jab drove, Ryder and Slick took off their jumpsuits. When Jab went around the corner, he slowed down enough for Ryder to get out. He let Slick out at the next corner and kept driving until he got to the parking garage where Ryder told him to hide the second vehicle. He moved the money to the clean vehicle and drove out.

19

That next morning, Meka and Gladys were meeting to make plans for a Big Night movie production, featuring Cristal. Prior to the meeting, Gladys made a call to Lola. "Gladys Gordon, Lola, how are you doing today?"

"I'm doing great, Gladys. How about you?"

"Doing great. Listen, I know this is short notice, but I was wondering if you could drop by the office today."

"Like you said, it is short notice, so I am not sure that my manager can be there."

"Oh, don't worry about that. This is informal, Lola. There are some things going on that I want to make you aware of."

"Okay," Lola said, and was very curious to know what Gladys could want to talk to her about. Her first thought was that they were getting ready to drop her. Not wanting to give any power to them, Lola quickly pushed those thoughts from her mind. "What time?"

"I'll be in the office all day; so come anytime." Gladys ended the call and was about to gather her things to go to meet with Meka, when there was a knock at the door.

"Mind if we meet in here?" Meka said and walked in Gladys's office.

"Not at all."

"I have been in my office since seven this morning and I just needed to get outta there."

"I know how that feels," Gladys said, and the meeting began in earnest.

At Meka's request, Gladys began with what could go wrong. "Everything. Not enough coverage, too much coverage, not enough usable coverage, artistic differences, bad performances from actors, money problems, finding a distributor for the film; the difficulty of going from initial concept to writing the screenplay."

"What is the most important part of a screenplay?" Meka asked.

"I'm told that it's the first fifteen minutes or the first fifteen pages," Gladys said. "A screenplay should pop on page one. Start with the story in motion, and that scene should foreshadow the story and the ending."

"I would have thought that the most important part of a movie is the last fifteen minutes," Meka commented.

As the meeting went on, Gladys talked with Meka about the five phases of film production. "The first phase is development. Generally, it takes up to three years; five to seven years for an independent production to go from script to package."

"Package?"

"Packaging is the process of getting a screenplay written, attaching stars to the project, as well as a director, producer, editor and distributor," Gladys shared.

"Okay. Now, is there any way that we can shave some time off that three to seven year time frame for an independent film?"

"Three words: money, money and money. You can do anything if you have enough money."

"What kinds of movies will the typical big-studio exec green light?"

Gladys shook her head. "Formula movies that target their main audience demographic: twelve to twenty-four year old white males, hot package deals with major stars, or an Alist director or producer is usually enough to get them interested."

"Where do big-studio execs get their material?"

"Adaptation of best sellers, reworking of old films, sequels, copy-cat films, TV spin-offs, comic books, and foreign remakes."

"Why is that?"

"Audience recognition."

Meka laughed. "What? No original work?"

"Not usually."

"And why is that?"

"To minimize their financial risk."

"Of course."

"But even though we may be able to attract a studio to a Cristal project, I think that going Indie is the best way for us."

Gladys then went on to explain that pre-production generally takes up to four months, and involved things like location scouting, story boards, production schedules, getting permits and setting the budget. The shooting phase can take ten to twelve weeks. And the post-production can take up to six months.

Just then, Gladys's phone rang and she put the call on speaker. "Gladys Gordon."

"I have Lola Frazier here to see you."

Gladys glanced at Meka; she nodded her head that it was cool.

"Escort her in."

Minutes later, Gladys's personal assistant showed Lola to the office. "Come in and have a seat," Gladys began.

"I want you to know that I am so sorry that we all haven't had a chance to get together and talk," Meka said. "I don't want you to think that it's because we have changed our plans or that our level of commitment to you, Lola."

"I'm sure that you've been wondering why Cristal, The Regulators and P Harlem are on tour and you're here playing club dates," Gladys said.

"You're right, Gladys. I really have been wondering what was up with that," Lola said.

"I know that you've made some changes to your act. I know that you hired a personal trainer, a costume designer and a chorographer to work on your performance. I wanted to be sure that you were ready before we sent you out on tour."

"How do you think all that's going?" Meka asked.

"I think it's going very well. But don't take my word for it. Come check out the show one night."

"I have," Meka said.

"I've been in the house every time you've gone onstage, Lola," Gladys said.

"Your show at Conversations was great, Lola," Meka said and looked at Gladys. "I think she's ready."

"I do, too," Gladys said and looked at Lola. "Let me share with you some of what we have planned," Gladys said.

"Okay, I'm listening," Lola said. She was playing it hard, but inside, she was jumping for joy.

"Their tour is winding down, so Paul and Monte will be coming back to cut a track together. Paul has plans to start on a studio album and once it's done, he is going back on tour. We want you to open for him."

"That's exactly what I wanted to hear."

I CAME TO BRING THE PAIN

"In fact, I spoke with Paul yesterday and he expressed an interest in working on some music with you."

"Really?"

"Yes. Have you ever met Paul?"

"I was introduced to him at the after-party at Impressions on the night Cuisine reopened."

Although she wouldn't consider herself a fan, Lola had been an admirer of P Harlem's work for a long time. After they were introduced that night, Lola was checking Paul out. But that was when she met Kayo.

"He is anxious to talk to you about the project, so we would like you to fly down to Atlanta this evening and go to the show," Gladys said.

"Tonight?"

Lola had once again arranged to meet Kayo. Unfortunately, the last few times they made plans, Kayo was a no-show. Afterwards, he would always have some excuse why he didn't make it and each time, he would promise that it wouldn't happen again. But Lola was growing tired of it.

"Will I get to perform?" Lola asked, hoping to hear the answer that she wanted.

"Yes, Lola. We arranged for you to do two songs. The first song you did with The Regulators and your latest."

"What time is my flight?" Lola asked excitedly.

"Your flight leaves at four this afternoon and arrives in the ATL at six-forty."

20

When Lola left the office, she was walking on air. She felt like she was back, or at least like she was on her way. The news she had just gotten was something that she wanted to share with Kayo, so she called him. Lola was surprised when he answered his phone.

"What's up, Lola."

"Me, wanting you."

"I want you, too."

"I have something to tell you, but I want to tell you in person."

"I don't think I like where this conversation is going."

"It's nothing bad." She paused. "I'm on my way home and I'll be there until about one. Can you come by?"

"I'll be there," Kayo said, but at one thirty, Lola had gotten tired of waiting for Kayo to get there and left for the airport.

That night in Atlanta, The Regulators opened for Cristal. At a designated time in the show, there would be some commotion and then the police would escort P Harlem, whose real name was Paul Roberts, to the stage. Each night, he'd call Monte out and the two would go at it. Then P Harlem would come up onstage, and after a fair amount of pushing and shoving, they would perform together.

While they were on tour, Paul and Monte got close. Each had a genuine respect for the other, and now they were actually becoming friends. They had talked about doing more than just the one song together and had begun writing lyrics and sampling beats that they might want to use.

After they went at it onstage, they would hang out, talk shit, and get fucked up off liquor and weed at the after-party. Paul passed Monte the blunt and sipped his drink. "Who do you think it will be tonight?"

Monte looked around at the men at the party. Monte took a hit. "That one," he said and pointed.

"He looks like her type," Paul began. "But my money's on the one in the blue."

"For how much?"

"A grand, like we always do."

"I thought you might want to make it easy on yourself." Monte passed the blunt back to Paul.

"You sound like a man that ain't confident in his pick."

"It's not that; but we'll find out soon enough. The diva queen is here," Monte said as Cristal made a grand entrance.

Cristal was an extremely talented, fierce, but often temperamental singer. But to others, Cristal was a bitchy woman that must have her way exactly, or no way at all. She was often rude and had a nasty habit of belittling people. Cristal was at her best, selfish, spoiled, and overly dramatic at times.

"I am not just some no-talent pop singer."

Her name was Chanta Malone. She was discovered and signed to Big Night by Gladys. Her album, which was released under her own name, did absolutely nothing. At that point, Fuller wanted to drop her, but Gladys stood steadfast. It was Gladys who suggested changing Chanta's name to Cristal.

"Why?" she asked.

"Because Cristal is the brand name of a champagne produced by Louis Roederer."

"So."

"It represents the embodiment of elegance. And awareness of its high price has given it an image of exclusivity that has elevated the demand for it," Gladys explained.

"I see where you're going with that."

After she had her name legally changed to Cristal, Gladys repackaged her image and began marketing her and her forthcoming album, even though she hadn't started on it.

Cristal was at times very domineering and excitable, but her talent permitted her to get away with that behavior. She wasn't necessarily difficult to work with; she was just very professional and had a low tolerance for any incompetence.

While on tour, at the after-parties, Cristal would pick up and fuck a different man every night, just not Paul or Monte. Each night, the two would make a bet on which man Cristal would leave the party with.

That night, Paul won the bet, because an hour after she arrived at the party, Cristal left with the man in the blue. "Pay up," he said with his hand out.

"Lucky guess," Monte said and reached in his pocket, peeled off a grand and handed it to Paul.

"Pleasure doing business with you."

It was well after midnight when Lola finally arrived at the after-party. She was wearing a St. John four-pocket knit blazer, long sleeve turtleneck and Santana knit pants.

"There she is," Monte said when he saw her. Lola came over to where Monte and Paul were sitting. "What happened to you?"

"I messed around and missed my flight. I hope I didn't cause too many problems with the show?" Lola asked.

"No. Not at all. We were just wondering what happened to you," Monte said, and then looked at Paul. "You know P Harlem, right?"

"Please, call me Paul," he said and extended his hand. "Good to see you again, Lola."

"Good to see you again, too."

Paul smiled at Lola. "How are you doing?"

"I'm good. A little tired from the flight and all, but I'm good."

"Can I get you something to drink?" Monte asked as he got up.

"Tequila Sunrise, please," Lola said to Monte, but she was still looking at Paul.

Monte saw the way they were looking at each other. "I'll leave you two alone to talk."

"I don't know if Gladys told you, but I've been working on something for us."

"Let me hear it," Lola said.

Paul began to rap what he had written and told Lola what parts were hers.

"I like this," she said and began trying to get her parts down.

It didn't take long before the people at the party were clapping their hands while Paul and Lola did what would be their new song.

It was then that Cristal returned to the party. She could hear the rapping and hand clapping as soon as she came through the door. She recognized P Harlem's distinctive sound right away, but not the female rapping with him.

91

When Cristal entered the room and saw that it was Lola, she got mad. She didn't like Lola and was well aware that the feeling was mutual. As soon as they were finished and the people at the party started clapping, Cristal let go in the highest soprano octave she could hit, and then she began to scat. Once she was done with her melody, the people in attendance all stood up and clapped for Cristal and she took her bows while looking dead at Lola.

"Show off," Monte said.

"I hate that bitch," Lola said.

It was almost one when Kayo walked in the diner and sat down at the counter. He looked out the corner of his eye at the man in the last booth. His name was Louis Juffe. He was an enforcer for Lloyd Brill and he also controlled some number banks. As the war with Black progressed, Brill had Juffe start recruiting more soldiers. But with things starting to turn against Brill, Juffe secretly reached out to Rain about switching sides.

"If he'll turn on Brill, he'll turn on us," Rain said. "Kill him."

That night, Juffe was having pie and coffee with some of the men that he had recruited. As the men talked, Treach came in the diner. He drew his weapon, walked right up to the table and shot Juffe in the chest. Kayo stood up and fired twice, hitting one of the men at the table with Juffe, and then Treach shot the other.

As the customers watched in horror, the two gunmen moved toward the door. Just then, another man came out of the restroom. He saw that his friends seated in the booth were dead and pulled out his gun.

"Hey!" he shouted and opened fire as Treach and Kayo headed for the door. Kayo turned quickly, aimed his gun and fired one shot at the man's head, and then they left the diner.

"I could use a drink," Treach told Kayo as they got in the car.

"Just one, and then I gotta go meet Lola," Kayo said and started the car. "I know you wanna go to Cynt's, so I ain't even gotta ask."

"So what's up with you and Lola Luv anyway?" Treach asked as they drove.

"Me and Lola are just cool."

"Yeah, right. Lola a little too damn fine for y'all to be just cool."

Kayo smiled and didn't comment.

"Yeah, nigga, you fuckin' Lola."

When the men got to Cynt's, they had a drink. Two hours, six drinks, Xtina, Coolie, Shay, Caviar, Philly Vanna, Candy, Ivory and Babydoll later, Kayo got up. "I gotta go meet Lola."

"Whatever," Treach said as Ivory and Babydoll danced for him.

"Looks like I'm cuttin' out at the right time."

"Why you say that?"

"There goes Maserati." Kayo pointed at a dancer with long straight, jet black hair coming out of the VIP area. With the exception of whatever footwear she was wearing, Maserati was always naked.

When Kayo made it to her, he told her that Treach was there waiting for her, and then he pointed in his direction. Maserati was a twenty-four year old dancer that stood five feet five inches tall and weighed 150 pounds, with measurements of 42-26-38.

And yes, her breasts were natural.

Maserati had enchanted Treach with those titties, her rich brown skin and her seductive grey eyes. "The fact that she never bothers to put on clothes in here may have something to do with it, too," Treach told Kayo one night.

When he saw Maserati heading in his direction, Treach quickly paid and dismissed Ivory and Babydoll.

"Hey, Treach," Maserati said. She leaned forward and hugged him; her large breast resting against his chest. "Your boy told me you was here." Maserati sat down on his lap and began grinding her hips. "You want me to dance for you?" she whispered in his ear.

"Go ahead."

Maserati had been dancing for Treach non-stop for almost forty-five minutes. That wasn't all that for her, since Maserati didn't do much actual dancing. She didn't have to. All Maserati had to do was step from side to side, shake her titties in her clients face, and then she'd turn around and bounce her ass. That was enough to make her the highest paid dancer at Cynt's.

A position formally held by Mercedes.

"But I ain't mad," Mercedes had said about Maserati. "You know I'll get mine. And I'll do it without selling this pussy to these niggas."

It was then that both Treach and Maserati saw Bootz. She was the exact opposite of Maserati. Where Maserati was all tits, Bootz was all ass. Her measurements were 34-28-47. She was a tall, slim redbone with short bleach-blonde hair.

Bootz had only been dancing at Cynt's for three weeks, but in that short period of time, she was quickly becoming a house favorite. And during that time, Bootz had caught the attention of not only Treach, but Maserati as well.

"Why don't you go get her? I know you want her," Treach said.

Maserati looked at him. Since he was right—she did want Bootz—Maserati went and got her. It didn't take long before Bootz was naked and both women were dancing for

Treach. When Maserati and Bootz began grinding their bodies against one another, Treach smiled.

"Maserati! Kiss her."

Bootz and Maserati both stopped and looked at Treach. Then they faced each other. Maserati grabbed Bootz's ass and pulled her toward her. Bootz took Maserati's face in her hands and kissed her passionately.

"I think we need to take this to the VIP," Treach said and stood up. Bootz picked up her clothes and both women followed him to the VIP area.

Meanwhile, outside the gambling house, three of Gee Cameron's men waited for one of Cynt's men to get back. When they saw the big man coming, two of them fell in behind him and pulled down their masks as they approached the door. He stepped inside and pressed the barrel of his gun into the big man's back. Big man started to reach for his gun.

"Try it, big boy," one whispered in his ear. "I wanna put a bullet in the back of your head." The big man moved his hand away from his gun. "Smart man. Now, open that door."

The big man unlocked the door and entered Cynt's with the three gunmen right behind him. They forced the big man to take them to Cynt's office. When they got to the office, they found Cynt and one of her men. One of Cameron's men put his foot in the big man's back and kicked him to the floor. Cynt jumped up when they came in.

"Everybody freeze!"

"What's this about?" she asked.

"Murder," he said and shot Cynt's man. Then one of the men raised his weapon and shot Cynt in the head.

Once they were in the room, the women started dancing for Treach. But it didn't take long for things to change. Maserati stood up on the couch and lowered herself onto Treach's face. He made circles around her clit. Bootz crawled between Treach's legs and undid his pants. Bootz reached between her thighs and fingered her clit with one hand, and took him into her mouth while she squeezed her nipple.

Treach very deliberately spread Maserati's lips and sucked her clit, but the whole time, she was looking over her shoulder at Bootz and couldn't wait to get at her. Treach slid his tongue inside her and sucked her moist lips gently.

Maserati watched as Bootz glided her hands across his dick and slowly begin to stroke it. Then Bootz put a condom on Treach, straddled his torso and eased herself down on him. She slid up and down on his dick as Maserati repositioned herself on Treach's face so she could watch.

Now Maserati and Bootz were facing each other and they started kissing. Bootz may have been flat chested, but what little she had was all nipples. Maserati squeezed Bootz's nipples while they explored each other's bodies. Treach licked and sucked Maserati's dripping wet pussy and pushed himself as deep as he could inside Bootz.

Then both women stopped and got off of Treach. Bootz lay across the couch and Maserati got between her legs. Bootz felt her body quiver as Maserati licked her clit with the tip of her tongue. She sucked Bootz's clit and it grew harder. Treach looked down at Maserati's ass up in the air and got in behind her, held onto her hips, and slammed into her.

Treach was fucking Maserati hard and fast when he heard gunshots. He pulled out of Maserati and put his pants on. As he got his guns, Treach had to shake his head.

"Damn, Maserati, you eating the hell out that pussy," he said as he left the VIP.

Once he saw the three armed men coming out of Cynt's office, Treach opened fire with both guns. They returned fire and began running for the door. As customers and dancers alike dove for the floor, the rest of Cynt's men began firing at the men and all three men died in the crossfire.

Once things quieted down and got back to some semblance of normal, Treach noticed that he hadn't seen Cynt since the shooting. He and one of Cynt's men went to the office to check on her, and that is when they found the bodies.

Cynt was dead.

23

One night, Black put in a call to Victor. At the time, he was seated at the bar at Upstairs; the Kimberly Hotel's penthouse level bar and lounge, with Jada. During the call, Black told Victor that he wanted to speak to Jada. "Bring her to Flip's spot."

"I'll take care of it," Victor said and went to Jada's table.

"Yes, Victor, what is it?"

"Sorry to bother you, Ms. West, but Mr. Black wants to talk to you."

Jada laughed. "Oh, really? And just where does Mr. Black want this conversation to take place?"

"He wants me to bring you to the spot that I used to run for him."

"Does he really?" Jada smiled and signaled for the waitress. "Well you tell Mr. Black that I am very busy this evening and I will make every effort to try to meet with him there tomorrow. If my schedule permits, of course."

"Of course," Victor said as the waitress arrived at the table.

"Another French 75, Ms. West."

"Please." As the waitress left the table, Jada looked at Victor. "Aren't you going to give Mr. Black my message?"

"Do you really want me to tell him that?"

"Yes, Victor. I want you to tell Mr. Black that I said that I am much too busy to meet him tonight."

"Okay." Victor returned to the bar and called Black to deliver Jada's message.

"She said what?"

"She said to tell you that she is much too busy to meet you tonight."

"Is she really? What is she too busy doing?"

"Sitting in her usual spot, pitching French 75's like they're water."

"When does Ms. West think that she'll have time to meet me?"

"She said that she will make every effort to try and meet with you there tomorrow. If her schedule permits, of course."

"Of course," he said angrily. "Well you tell Ms. West," Black began and then he got calm. "You tell Ms. West I said okay. She can meet me whenever she has the time." Black ended the call.

It was two days later when Jada decided that she was ready to talk to Black. Since she'd been in the city, Jada had recruited six new ladies, and four of them were already working. While she looked for a spot to setup the new establishment, which Jada had been calling Paraíso North; Simone had taken control of the ladies.

Jada was still training the two new ladies, Zacaria and Chloe, so she decided to bring them along. Then she told Victor to call to reserve a limousine for them to ride to the gambling spot. When they arrived, the driver got out and came around to the back door. The driver stood by the door as Victor got out and stood next to the driver.

Zacaria got out first and stood next to Victor. She was wearing a Roberto Cavalli beaded-border sheath dress. Chloe got out looking amazing in her Burberry London lace dress. Then the driver extended his hand for Jada. She was dressed flawlessly in her Akris embroidered insert dress with sheer tulle inserts embroidered with a zebra-inspired pattern.

The entrance of three beautiful and impeccably dressed ladies did not go unnoticed by the assembled gamblers at the spot. Jada scanned the room quickly, but didn't see Black anywhere. Victor showed Jada to a table; she sat down and her new ladies stood behind her. Then Victor excused himself and went to the office and knocked on the door. Flip opened the door for Victor and he went in to find Black, Rain, Jackie and Sonny Edwards seated in the office.

"What's up, Victor? She with you?" Black asked.

"She's sitting outside."

"Who?" Rain wanted to know.

"Jada West. I want her to recruit the women to work here."

When Black stood up, Rain did too, and then she followed him out of the office. Jada watched as Black came out of the office. But what was more important to her was who came out with him. Naturally, she'd met Rain.

Some people you just don't forget.

From what Victor had told Simone, Jada assumed the woman was Jackie and the younger man was Flip. But it was the older gentlemen that peeked Jada's attention. She watched as Sonny sat down at the table and they dealt him in.

The closer Black got to Jada, the stronger the urge to fuck her silly got inside him. Black pushed those urges to the side and walked to her table.

"Good evening, Mr. Black. Please have a seat."

Rain stood behind Black as he sat across from Jada. "How are you, Ms. West?"

"I am absolutely fantastic."

"You look nice this evening, Ms. West."

"Why thank you, Mr. Black. That was very kind of you to say."

"You're welcome."

"Please permit me to introduce you to Zacaria Patton and Chloe Bailey. Ladies, this is Mr. Black."

"Good evening, Mr. Black," the ladies both said.

"Nice to meet you, ladies."

"Would you ladies excuse us?"

"Yes, Jada."

Jada glanced at Rain and then to Black. He nodded once, and without having to be told, Rain walked away and left Black alone with Jada.

"So, Mr. Black." Jada paused and leaned forward. "To what do I owe the privilege of this audience that you have so graciously granted me?"

"I need you to recruit some women to work here."

Jada smiled and was happy because he needed her, and that was really all she wanted.

Well, not really all I want from him, but we'll pass that point for now, shall we?

"Not a problem, Mr. Black. Just tell me how many ladies that you would like and how soon you'd like them."

"Four or five. And I need them as soon as possible."

"You are welcome to Zacaria and Chloe, and I will have the others here within the week. Is that acceptable?"

"Yes, it is."

"Will there be anything else?"

"No, Ms. West, that's all I needed."

Jada stood up and looked at Victor and then to the ladies. "Well, if there's nothing else, I'll say good night, Mr. Black."

"Good night, Ms. West."

Black sat there and watched Jada as she walked out of the spot with Victor, Zacaria and Chloe following behind her. Rain came and sat down next to Black. He shook his head. "Come on, let's get outta here."

Later that night at Impressions, Gladys introduced Black to Scarlett Brock, an R&B artist that Gladys had discovered in Aruba; recently signed and brought to New York. "And wait until you see her dance," Gladys told Black.

"It's good to meet you, Mr. Black," Scarlett said.

Black noticed her accent. "Where are you from, Mrs. Brock?"

"I am from St. Vincent," Scarlett answered and saw the look on Black's face. "Have you ever heard of it?"

Black smiled. "Not only have I heard of it, I was born in St. Vincent."

"Really?"

"My mother was born and raised there before she moved us to New York. Next time I talk to her I will have to ask her if she knows any Brock's."

"Brock is my married name, Mr. Black. My madden name is Laurent."

Black looked at Scarlett. "Is Fenton Laurent your father?"

"Yes. But how did you know that?"

Black looked at Gladys. "Come with me, Mrs. Brock. You and I have a lot to talk about," Black said and began to walk toward Bobby's office.

Scarlett gave Gladys a confused look. "Go with him," she said, and Scarlett rushed off to catch up with Black.

When they got to the office, Tara, who had managed Impressions for years, was seated behind the desk. "Evening, Tara."

"Hey, Mike," Tara said and smiled until she saw Scarlett come in behind him.

"Tara, I would like to introduce you to Mrs. Scarlett Brock. She is the latest edition to Big Night Records."

"Nice to meet you, Mrs. Brock."

"Tara, I need the room for a minute," Black said, and Tara got up and left the office.

"Have a seat, Mrs. Brock," Black said after Tara left. "Can I get you something?"

"No, thank you."

Black sat down in the chair next to Scarlett. "This is awkward." He paused. "I've been to St. Vincent before many years ago. I paid some people a lot of money to be introduced to your father. He showed me a picture of his wife, his two sons and his daughter. He was so proud of you."

"Now, I *am* curious, Mr. Black."

"Please call me Mike."

"Only if you stop calling me Mrs. Brock." Scarlett laughed. "Every time you call me that, I keep looking around for my mother-in-law." Both Black and Scarlett laughed. "But, Mike, I am curious about why you paid to meet my father?"

"Because I wanted to meet *my* father."

"What did you say?"

"My mother told me that Fenton Omar Laurent is my father." Black paused. "So, Scarlett, I am your brother."

Black told Scarlett how his mother and their father met and got together one night at the dancehall.

"She said that she didn't know him before that night. Only thing she could remember about him was that he was kind of arrogant."

Scarlett laughed. "She would not be the first person to say that about Daddy."

"By the way, is he still a cop?" Black asked.

"No," Scarlett said quickly and changed the subject, because it was something that she didn't want to get into with him. "Now that I'm looking at you, you do look like him."

"It was funny when I met him; the way he kept looking at me." Black laughed. "He kept sayin' how familiar I looked to him. That's when he broke out the family pictures."

"Why didn't you tell him that he was your father?"

"I mean biologically he is, but he's not. I mean, by no real fault of his own, he wasn't a father to me. I don't hold it against him."

Scarlett reached in her purse and handed Black a picture. "Your niece and nephew, Uncle Mike."

"What are their names?"

"My daughter's name is Sherraine and my son is Gordy."

"My wife and I have a daughter and a son, too. Her name is Michelle; my son is Mike Jr., but we call him Easy."

Just then, Bobby burst through the door. He was about to say something when he saw Scarlett in the office with Black. "Bobby," Black said excitedly. "There's somebody I want you to meet. Bobby, this is Scarlett Brock. She's my sister."

"Nice to meet you," Bobby said and then he realized what Black had said. "What did you say, Mike?"

"Scarlett is my sister."

Bobby shook his head. "It really is nice to meet you but, Mike, we really need to talk."

Black looked at Bobby and had known him long enough to know that there was something wrong. And whatever it was, it was bad.

"Scarlett, would you excuse me for a minute."

"No problem, Mr. Black. I mean, Mike." She got up. "It was nice to meet you, too, Bobby," Scarlett said as she left the office.

"What's wrong?"

"Cynt is dead."

When Black and Bobby left the office and walked into the club, they walked right past Agent McCullough. She was just about to present herself to security and ask to be seen, but this seemed a bit more promising.

"Rain," Black said when he found her at the bar.

"What's up, Black?"

"I need you to come with us."

"What's wrong?"

"Cynt is dead."

When they arrived at Cynt's, they had moved the bodies out of sight and the spot was back up and running. Treach took Black, Bobby and Rain to where they had taken the bodies. Rain looked at the men.

"Those is Gee Cameron's people."

"Where can I find that mutha fucka?" Bobby asked. Back in the day, he and Cynt had a little thing going for a minute. Even though it was long since over and done with, Bobby still wanted to avenge her death.

"I know somebody that might be able to tell us."

"Who?" Black asked. He and Cynt had been in business together since the old days. And even though he felt betrayed by her for backing Wanda when she moved against Nick, Black still had love for Cynt.

"Nigga named Lee Gilbert."

"Let's go," Black said and then he turned to Treach. "You stay here and take charge of this place."

Black walked away. Treach smiled and Rain got in his face. "This is your spot until I say different." Rain put her finger in his chest. "So don't fuck it up," she said and rushed to catch up with Black.

Treach watched Rain walk away and then he noticed that Bobby was still standing there. "That means you're here to do more than just fuck Maserati's big tittie havin' ass."

On the way out, Black stopped to talk to Mercedes. She quickly told Black everything that she knew and had seen that night. Before they left, Rain told her that Treach would be running things there. "So you help him."

Mercedes smiled at Rain as she walked away. She knew Rain couldn't stand her because of Nick, but Mercedes never cared. Rain had just handed her a present; one that let her know that the spot would soon be hers.

On their way to Lee Gilbert's apartment, Rain had questions. "You remember when I sent Spence and them after Balendin and you said that you and me gotta learn to take a step back and let our people do the work?"

"I remember what I said," Black said.

"Probably told you some shit about you being too valuable to risk losing you," Bobby said.

Rain laughed. "That's what he said."

"When it's personal, all that shit goes out the window," Bobby said.

"And killin' Cynt is personal," Black said.

"I'm just askin'." Rain smiled. "But now I got another question."

"What's that?"

"I don't mean to question you, Black, but why you leave Treach in charge?"

"It's a test," Black said.

"You and them damn tests." Bobby shook his head.

"You told me that Treach was a good man, but he loves pussy and he's weak for Maserati."

"You wanna see what he'll do. Be about business or that pussy," Rain said.

"It was a test for you."

"Did I pass?"

"Right away. I wanted to see how long it took for you to understand that Treach wasn't ready for that, and put Mercedes in charge. And I really am interested to see how long it takes for Mercedes to takeover and how she goes about it. Mercedes has turned out to be a lot smarter than I thought she was."

"Yeah," Bobby laughed. "She's definitely not dumber than a box of rocks."

"What y'all talking about?"

"When she first started working there, Mike told me that she was fine, but Mercedes was dumber than a box of rocks," Bobby said and everybody laughed.

"That was clearly an act," Rain said, and then thought about Mercedes and Nick. "Because Mercedes is one sneaky bitch."

26

When they got there, Bobby kicked the door in. Lee was in there with Titus Wallace; they both grabbed their guns and began firing. Black, Bobby and Rain moved to opposite sides of the door and waited for them to run out of bullets. Once Lee and Titus were empty, they went inside the apartment.

Titus ran in the back room and Bobby went in after him and was able to get to Titus before he could reload. Bobby grabbed Titus and punched him in the face again and again. Then he punched him in the stomach and dragged him back in the living room.

By that time, Black and Rain had subdued Lee and had him sitting in the middle of the floor with his hands on his head and Rain standing over him. Bobby pushed Titus and he stumbled to the floor. Rain kicked him in the face. "Get up on your knees, hands on your head," she demanded.

Black knelt down on the floor next to Lee. "I'm gonna asked you one question. Tell me what I want to know and Rain won't kill you."

Rain put her gun to Lee's head.

"Where can I find Gee Cameron?"

"I ain't tellin' you shit," Lee said defiantly.

"Rain."

Rain pulled the trigger. "I always love rollin' wit' you niggas."

Black saw the look on Titus's face. Then he looked at Rain and smiled. "Open the window, Rain."

Rain smiled and went to the window and opened it.

"What y'all gonna do?" Titus needed to know.

"We're gonna drop you out that window," Rain said. "But don't worry, we do this kinda shit all the time and we're good at it." She laughed and put her gun to his head. "Get up."

When Titus didn't move, Black and Bobby picked him up and carried him to the window.

"Y'all ain't gotta do this!" he yelled.

Rain walked alongside of him. "Tell me what I wanna know and you won't have to fuckin' worry about getting dropped out the window."

"Okay, okay, I'll tell you where he is."

Black and Bobby put him down slowly. "Now, you was gonna tell me where your boy Gee Cameron is," Rain said.

"He's at his woman's house."

"Thank you," Bobby said, and then he shot Titus in the back of the head.

Now that they knew where Gee Cameron was, Black, Bobby and Rain left the apartment and headed in that direction. When they got there, Bobby spotted a man coming out of the house.

"That's Jordan Barrett," Rain said. "He's Gee's bagman."

"Not anymore," Bobby said and got out of the car.

Barrett had just made it to his car and had opened the door, when Bobby walked up behind him and put two in the back of his head.

When they approached the house, they saw four men out in front. Black, Bobby and Rain took out their guns and opened fire on Cameron's men. They were caught completely off guard and when the shooting stopped, all four of Cameron's men were dead.

113

Black, Bobby and Rain went into the house and saw Henry Belcher. He had his gun out and began shooting. Cameron looked at Rain, smiled, and then he picked up his gun. He opened fire as he ran for the back door and Rain went after him.

Black and Bobby took cover, returned fire, and kept shooting until Belcher was out of bullets. Then they stood up and walked slowly toward Belcher. Rain came back in the room. "He got away."

"No worries, Rain. This man right here is gonna tell us where Cameron is hiding from us." Bobby punched Belcher in the face. "Where is Gee going?" Bobby said and punched him again.

"I don't know!" he shouted.

"Let me ask you something: is pain something you enjoy?" Black asked. "If not, I suggest that you tell us want we want to know."

"Understand?" Bobby said and punched him again.

Since Belcher wasn't talking, Bobby went to work on him while Black held him. While Bobby did his work, Rain sat down and watched them.

"Where's Gee going?" Black asked in between Bobby's punches.

Bobby punched him again. "Answer the man!"

By this time Belcher was bleeding from the mouth as a result of Bobby's work. He still didn't answer. After a while of taking that beating, Belcher's jaw along with two of his ribs had been broken, but he still wasn't talking.

"This is getting us nowhere," Black said and looked at Rain.

She stood up and walked over to Belcher. "You should have told them what they wanted to hear. But you didn't"—Rain put the barrel of her gun to his eye—"so now you're gonna die. You dumb ass mutha fucka." Then she pulled the trigger.

27

When Tyhedra walked into Bar Veloce on 7th Avenue, a few heads turned as she took a seat at the bar. She ordered a drink; and while she sipped, Tyhedra looked around the room and spotted her prey for the night. He was a tall, good-looking man and very well dressed.

After giving him the eye he sent her a drink, and Tyhedra motioned for him to join her. They talked for a while and then she suggested that they would be more comfortable at a table in the back of the bar. Once Tyhedra had him in a position where they wouldn't be noticed, it was time to go.

"So, tell me, what does a gorgeous woman like you have planned for the rest of the evening?"

She leaned close to him. "I plan to be naked and wet. Wanna come?"

"I definitely wanna come," he said excitedly.

"Why don't we get out of here," Tyhedra said and then she stood up quickly. But just as quickly, Tyhedra sat back down and turned away. "What is he doing here," she said quietly.

"What's wrong?"

"Don't look; but I used to date that guy in the black suit."

"You used to date that guy?"

"We broke up weeks ago."

Tyhedra gave her prey her helpless and defenseless look. She had run that routine many times before. The objective was to not be seen leaving the bar with her prey.

"Look, I don't want him to see us together. It will only cause a scene and I'm not in the mood for that tonight."

"I understand."

"Why don't you wait for me outside? I promise I won't be long."

"Okay." He stood up. "I'll be outside," he said, and Tyhedra watched as her prey for the evening walked off.

When Tyhedra came out of the Veloce she looked around and saw him standing by a car. "I was starting to think that you changed your mind."

The predator bared her teeth at her prey. "There was no chance of that happening."

"So what now?"

"You lead and I'll follow," Tyhedra said. "Where is your car?"

"Right over there," he said and pointed.

"Good. I'll follow you."

She followed him to the Liberty Inn on 10th Avenue and waited in the car until he paid for the room. When he came out, Tyhedra pretended to be on the phone.

"Why don't you go ahead and get ready for me, baby." She held up the phone. "I'll be up in a minute."

The prey told her what room he was in and then Tyhedra waited until she saw him go in before she started up her car and drove down the street. She parked her car and came back on foot. Once Tyhedra had satisfied herself that there was nobody around that could identify her, she made her way to the room and knocked on the door.

"Take off your clothes," Tyhedra said as soon as she walked in the room.

As quickly as he could, the prey took off his clothes and stood there watching as Tyhedra unzipped her dress and let it drop to the floor. Then she reached behind her back, unhooked her bra, and slid it off her shoulders.

"You are so damn fine," the prey said as he stroked himself.

Once she was naked, Tyhedra told him to sit down on the bed and she sat next to him. She let him run his hand across her breasts and then he teased them with his tongue. He slid his tongue slowly around her nipples while Tyhedra spread her legs and fingered her clit. Very slowly and seductively, she got on her knees took his length in her hands and stroked it.

"You like this, baby?"

"Yes," the prey moaned.

"I wanna suck your dick," Tyhedra said softly. Then she took the head in her mouth, while she continued to finger herself.

Once Tyhedra had her fill of sucking his dick, she stood up.

"Where you going?" he asked frantically.

"I'll be right back," Tyhedra said.

She grabbed her purse and went into the bathroom. When she came out, Tyhedra had on a pair of plastic gloves and a long scarf wrapped around her body. Tyhedra danced back to the bed and carefully placed her purse on the nightstand before getting back in bed with him.

Tyhedra put a condom on her prey; and then she straddled his body, grabbed his dick, and slid down on it. She began to move her body up and down on him, and he grabbed her ass and began pumping it to her.

I CAME TO BRING THE PAIN

Tyhedra rode him slowly and then she began to pull the scarf slowly away from her body. Once it was off of her, Tyhedra tied his hands to the bed frame while she continued to fuck him slowly. Once his bonds were tied tight, she began to move her body faster. The prey closed his eyes and began to thrust his body into hers. Tyhedra got off of him and tied his ankles to the frame. Then she got his belt and came back to the bed.

Tyhedra looked at her prey. "We're gonna have some fun now." Tyhedra laughed a little. "Well—at least I am."

She crawled up on the bed again and slowly slid the belt around his neck and looped it through the buckle. Then Tyhedra pulled on the end of it and kept pulling until it was tight, just not tight enough to strangle him.

With a firm grip on the belt, she grabbed his dick and slowly lowered herself on him. Tyhedra rode him slowly at first while she pulled tighter and tighter on the belt. She fucked him harder and pulled tighter. Then Tyhedra grabbed the belt with both hands and pulled as hard as she could. Her prey began to struggle against it and his body stiffened. Tyhedra screamed as he stopped moving and then she exhaled.

28

The next morning, Carmen Taylor had just locked the door to her apartment when the phone began to ring. She put her things down and rushed to pick it up before it went to voice mail. Carmen glanced at the display and saw that it was Detective Diane Mitchell calling. "Hey, Diane."

"Hey, Carmen, and before you ask, the answer is yes."

"He wants to go public," Carmen said excitedly.

"Not exactly. The mayor decided that they don't want or need the media attention they would get if they arrested a serial killer."

"Better to keep up the safe-city front," Carmen said, and then she thought about it. "If he decided not to go public, what answer is yes?"

"What's yes is that somehow that information will reach the press anyway. So, with that in mind, why don't you and Max meet me at the Liberty Inn on 10th Avenue?"

Liberty Inn was the mother of all hourly hotels. The rooms are pretty basic, but they all have mirrors and mood lighting, a colossal porn collection, and a exercise pad, which was a triangular block of foam that a lady can lie back on to elevate her hips for extra pleasure. There was even a romantic interlude room where couples can get busy in the Jacuzzi.

When Carmen arrived with Max, they didn't waste any time getting to work. While Max and the film crew got set up, Carmen began working the crowd. She was interviewing one of the people in the crowd, when she spotted a woman standing off in the distance looking at her. Judging solely by the way the woman was dressed, Carmen assumed that she was a working girl.

After a while, it became clear that the woman was waiting to talk to Carmen. She was just about to walk over there to see what the woman wanted when Detective Mitchell came out of the hotel. Carmen looked at the woman; they made eye contact, and then she rushed off to catch the detective.

"What can you tell us about the victim in this crime, Detective?" Carmen shouted over the other reporters who had received an anonymous tip that this was an active crime scene.

"No comment," Mitchell said as she passed the reporters.

"Was the victim really tied to the bed and strangled?"

Mitchell stopped and looked at Carmen. "I have no comment." Then Mitchell walked away just as they had planned it.

After things settled down and most of the reporters had left the crime scene, Carmen noticed that the woman was still standing there. She walked over to her. "You're Carmen Taylor, right?"

"Yes, I am."

"I thought so," the woman said excitedly.

"What's your name?"

"Frenchy."

"Do you know anything about what happened here today?"

"I think I might have seen the woman that did it."

Carmen dug in her bag and took out the sketch that Mitchell had given her of the suspect. She showed it to the woman. "Is this her?"

The woman looked at the picture and then handed in back to Carmen. "That looks like her, except she was black."

"Wait, what did you say?"

"The woman I saw was black," Frenchy told Carmen again.

"Wait right there, okay? Don't go anywhere," Carmen said excitedly and rushed away. When she returned, Detective Mitchell was with her.

"This is Detective Mitchell, Frenchy."

"Hello, Frenchy. Why don't you tell me what you saw?"

"I was finished with my client and when I came out of the room, I saw a woman go in the room where they found the body."

Mitchell showed Frenchy the artist's sketch. "And you say this is the woman you saw going in the room?"

"That looks like her. But like I told Carmen Taylor, the woman I saw was black."

Mitchell and Carmen looked at one another and then back at Frenchy.

"Thank you for your help," Carmen said, and Frenchy started to walk away.

"I'm gonna need you to come with me," Mitchell said. The sketch that the detective had been showing was faxed to her from the LAPD and wasn't in color. Mitchell had assumed from looking at the sketch that her serial killer was a white female.

"Why?"

"I need to get you to talk to a sketch artist," Mitchell said.

"I can't go to no police station," Frenchy said and looked at Carmen.

"Can I speak to you for a second, Detective?"

The detective looked at Carmen and then to Frenchy, and walked away.

"What?"

"It's obvious that she is scared to go to the precinct because of some pimp."

"I know that, Carmen, but she is my only witness and I need an accurate sketch of the killer."

"Is there any way you could bring the sketch artist to her?"

"Okay, Carmen. You take her someplace safe and I'll bring the sketch artist to her."

"Thanks, Diane." Carmen said. "I'm still trying to wrap my mind around the fact that our killer is a black woman."

"I know, Carmen. The fact that she's black changes everything."

It took some time and a lot of convincing, but Shy was finally able to talk Pam out of the house. Since she almost died in the bombing at Impressions, Pam really hasn't left the house. The only place that she would go was to the grocery store, and that took months of the entire family going with her to feel comfortable.

That night, Pam and Shy went to a club called Joy on West 28th Street. Even though they didn't stay long, Shy was happy that Pam had actually made it out and that she seemed to have had a good time. It was a little after one in the morning when Napoleon let Pam out in front of her house and she went inside. Shy got in the front seat with Napoleon.

"I don't know about you, but I'm hungry," Shy said.

"With all due respect, Mrs. Black, when you know me not to be hungry?"

"Let's roll by Fat Larry's."

"Your wish is my command," Napoleon said and drove in that direction.

It was just then that Shy's cell rang. She looked at the display and saw that it was Black calling. "Hey, baby."

"You and Pam still hanging out?"

"I just dropped her off at home and now we're on our way to Fat Larry's to get some chicken and go home."

"Ain't it too late to be eating?"

"Yes, but we're hungry."

Black looked at Rain. "Roll by Fat Larry's."

"Good idea. I'm hungry."

"Stay there until we get there, Cassandra. We're on our way," Black said, and Rain headed in that direction.

When Shy and Napoleon got to Fat Larry's, they had to park around the corner. They walked back to the chicken and rib joint and went inside.

"What you gonna have?" Shy asked.

"I'm gon' have the grilled lamb gyro sandwich," Napoleon said. "What about you?"

Shy looked at the menu. "I was gonna have the grilled boneless chicken breast on pita bread, but I'm gonna have a fried fish fillet sandwich."

"Does the boss want anything?"

"Michael doesn't like to eat at this hour."

"More for us," Napoleon said and high-fived Shy.

When Black arrived with Rain, she double-parked in front of Fat Larry's and they went inside.

"What's up?"

"Order me a grilled chicken teriyaki sandwich," Rain said on her way to the ladies room.

"You want anything, Michael?"

"Y'all go ahead," Black said and sat down at the table with Shy and Napoleon while they waited for their food.

When the food was ready, Rain grabbed hers and said good night. "I'll get with you in the morning, Black," she said and got in her Lexus.

"I'll go get the car," Napoleon said and walked down the street.

Black wrapped his arm around Shy. "Did Pam have a good time tonight?"

"I think she did. At least she said she did. She even danced once, which by the way, is one time more than I hit the dance floor."

"You didn't feel like dancing?" Black asked as he leaned against a car.

"Didn't have my dance partner with me." Shy paused. "Do you realize that the last time we went dancing was in Saint-Tropez," she said and thought about the time they spent in the French Riviera.

"When all this is over, I promise to take you dancing every night for a month."

"I'm gonna hold you to that," Shy said, and was about to go and lean against the car next to Black when she saw a car coming at them fast. When the car began to slow down as it got closer, Shy thought it was Napoleon, until she saw two guns emerge from the front and back window on the passenger side.

"Look out, Michael!"

Black looked at the car and had just enough time to grab Shy and dive for the ground before the shooting started. But instead of the shooters driving by, they stopped the car. Four Hispanic men jumped out and continued firing at Black and Shy.

Black took out both of his guns while Shy dug in her purse for her Beretta. They opened fire on their attackers. Black fired and dropped back for cover. Shy rose up and fired twice. Both shots found their mark, and then she took cover. Black looked at her.

"This may not be the best time for this, but you know what I've noticed?" Black asked as the men kept firing.

Shy looked wide-eyed at Black. "What?"

Black came up firing and hit one of the men as he tried to get closer. "You're gettin' to be a better shot." He stood up and shot another.

Shy quickly hugged Black. "You noticed," she said, and then she came up firing again as the last man standing ran for the car. Shy stood up and took aim.

Sight picture—Trigger squeeze, Shy said the words her instructor always repeated to herself and squeezed the trigger. Shy hit the man in the back of the head while he was running.

"Good shooting, gangster," Black said as Napoleon brought the car to a screeching halt in front of them. Black opened the car door for Shy; they got in and Napoleon drove them home.

30

The following evening, Mileena was at Impressions getting her station ready for the evening. At first glance, Mileena appeared to be the epitome of femininity and she played the role well. But look deeper and you'll see that Mileena, with all her sweet mannerisms and lovely grace, was as tough as they came.

As the evening wore on and the drinks were flowing, Ice and Mitch entered the club. When Mileena saw both of them coming toward her station, she quickly grabbed a bottle and got very busy, very quickly making drinks. Once the two men passed the bar and made their way to the office, Mileena relaxed.

She hated it when they came in together. *They are friends, you know*, Mileena thought. She never intended to become physically involved with both Ice and Mitch, but that was exactly what she was doing. Mileena was fucking both of them and neither one knew about the other.

"At least I don't think they know," Mileena said.

Ryder shook her head. "Wasn't it you that told me not to get involved with these gangsters because they'll break my heart? Wasn't that you?"

"Yes, it was," Mileena admitted. She generally gave very good advice, though she seldom followed it. "And it wasn't like I was trying to get with two friends like that."

"So how'd it happen?"

"I met Mitch one week; took him home with me that night. I met the Ice man a couple of weeks later, we hung out and I went to a hotel with him," Mileena said. "Besides, men have been doing shit like that for years. They need to know what it feels like." There were times when she truly thought like a man and operated with a kind of male logic, but Mileena was smart enough to let the man think he was on top in every situation, when she was clearly running things her way.

"Only problem with that is one or both of them might kill your bighead ass if they find out. And then I gotta do something about it," Ryder said as Ice came toward the bar. "Hey, Ice," she said and picked up her drink.

"What's up, Ryder." Ice looked at Mileena. "How you doin', Mileena?"

Mileena placed a bar napkin in front of Ice. "What are you having?"

Ice smiled. "Surprise me."

"Gentleman Sour, coming up." Mileena turned quickly and mixed two parts Gentleman Jack, one part lemon juice, and one part syrup. She shook the ingredients and served the drink in a rock glass over ice, and garnished it with an orange slice and a cherry.

It was at that moment when Black and Shy came in Impressions along with Napoleon. When they walked by the dance floor, Black and Shy passed a table which was occupied by Agent McCullough.

That was when Shy looked at the bar and thought that she saw somebody that she knew. As Black headed for the office, Shy excused herself and headed for the bar. Mitch was on his way to speak to Mileena until he saw Shy and Napoleon heading for the bar. He turned quickly and went the other way. As soon as Ice saw her coming that way, he drained his glass, quickly said good-bye to the ladies, and walked away.

Shy walked up behind Ryder. "Dale?" Shy said and Ryder turned around slowly.

"No it ain't you, Sandy," Ryder said.

Ryder's real name was Dale, but when she was growing up, she was always teased because Dale was a boy's name. That ended the day that she got fed up with the teasing and started kicking ass.

"Why they call you Ryder, Dale?" Shy asked.

"When people ask me this, Sandy, I usually say, 'why you think?', but my. . ."—Ryder paused and thought for a second about her dead husband, Donaldo. ". . . my ex started calling me that." Shy looked at Ryder and started to laugh a little. "And before you bust up laughing, I'll tell you why."

"You mean other than the obvious, Dale—I mean, Ryder."

"Yeah, Sandy, other than the obvious." Ryder laughed and took a playful swing at Shy. "Back in the day when he was doing his thing, I was always right there with him."

Shy smiled. "So you a ride-or-die chick, huh?" she said and thought about how her and Black spent the last evening.

"You know I ain't changed, Sandy," Ryder said.

"I see."

"What about you? Last time I saw you, you was on your way to college."

"Damn, it has been that long." Shy shook her head. "I finished college; started my own business." Shy flashed her rings. "Got married; got a couple of kids."

"That's nice, Sandy."

I CAME TO BRING THE PAIN

Shy looked and saw Black coming with Rain. "Here he comes now."

Ryder's eyes opened wide when Black walked up and kissed Shy. "Hey, Baby."

"I gotta go somewhere with Rain. I won't be gone long."

"Want me to go with you?" Shy asked.

"It ain't that type of party, gangster."

"Okay," a disappointed Shy said as a still wide-eyed Ryder looked on. "Baby, I want you to meet an old friend of mine," Shy began and turned to Ryder. "This is—" she said and Black cut her off.

"Ryder, right?"

"Oh—you know her?"

"We've met."

Shy shook her head. "You do know everybody, don't you? Anyway, me and Ryder have known each other since junior high school."

Black glanced at Rain; she was pointing to her watch. "Good to see you again, Ryder. I know I'll see you again." He turned to Shy.

"Go, Michael," Shy said and Black kissed her. Then he rushed to catch up with Rain.

"That's your husband?"

"Yes," Shy smiled.

"You're Shy?" Ryder asked and pointed at Shy.

"I'm afraid so."

"I feel like I should drop to my knees and kiss them big ass rings. And what did he call you?"

"Gangster," Shy said proudly because she loved it when he called her that.

"Why does he call you that, Sandy?"

"'Cause I'm a ride-or-die chick, too, *Ryder*," Shy said, and the two old friends hugged one another.

Later that night, Black and Rain arrived at the warehouse that Sherman was operating out of. When they got there Sherman, as well as Bobby, were in the warehouse with Smoke.

"We gonna start going hard at Gee Cameron and Rob Berry, Sherman," Rain ordered.

"I hear you. We gotta hit 'hem hard for Cynt."

"Take it straight to them and don't let up," Black said.

"Since Rain blew up the Kings Restaurant, there's no one place that we can hit Gee," Sherman said.

"Rain taught him the value of floating," Bobby said.

"But that nigga Rob Berry is a different story. You can always find him at his place, Sweet Nectar," Sherman said.

"Only problem with that is that he got a fuckin' army of niggas up in there," Rain said.

"Rain," Black began, "I want you to focus your attention on catching Cameron. Put as many people as you need on it, but I want him found and I want him dead."

"I'll get him, Black," Rain promised.

"I know you will." Black looked at Sherman. "You need to find a way to get Rob Berry. You either find a way to get him outta there or send an army up in there to get him. This shit has gone on long enough."

Since Bobby was there, Rain felt comfortable leaving Black and going to take care of some business. She stood up. "I'm out, Black."

"You going to take care of that little matter?"

"Yeah, I'll get with you tomorrow."

"Around two," Black said.

"Come on, Smoke, you're with me."

After Rain and Smoke left the warehouse, Black's cell began to ring. It was the call from Miami that he'd been waiting for. Once he had all the information that he needed, Black ended the call. "That was my guy in Miami."

"Is he back?" Bobby asked.

"No, he's in Puerto Rico. He heard that I wanted to talk, so he invited Cassandra and I to come to Puerto Rico and be his guests at the St. Regis Bahia Beach Resort."

"When's he expecting you?"

"Anytime. We have a standing reservation. Just contact his people to let him know we're there."

"And you say he wants you *and* Shy to come down there?" Bobby said and smiled.

"Yeah, picture that if you will."

"Sounds like fun. Be sure to take plenty of pictures," Bobby said as Nick came in with Monika. When they saw Nick, everybody stood up. Black approached him first.

"Congratulations."

Nick glanced at Monika. "You told him?"

"He made me tell him," Monika said and walked away smiling as, one by one, each man congratulated Nick on his becoming a father.

"Thank you," Nick said and told them how he and April had gotten together at one of Black's party's.

"I bet a lotta babies got conceived at those parties," Sherman said as the memories of those nights filled his mind. "Yeah, those were some of the best parties."

"And he's sixteen years old," Bobby said. "He's the same age as RJ."

While the others talked and joked with Nick, Black thought back to those days. Some of his memories were good and some weren't. Black thought about Carmen and their brief but intense time together. It wasn't lost on him that it was then that Regina found out about Carmen and how serious he was about her. And even though Black had let Carmen go so she could become somebody, it marked the beginning of the end of his relationship with Regina. After that, they spiraled out of control.

Eager to change the subject, Nick sat down next to Black. "I heard you have something going on that me and Monika can help you with."

As he did with Monika, Black explained in detail what happened when Wanda took power and the results of it. "And that's why I need my two favorite assassins."

"You can count on us, Black," Nick said.

"Just tell me where to find them and it's done," Monika promised.

Black laid out the particulars for the two assassins of what he wanted done. "And I want it done tonight."

When Black was done, Nick asked Black if they could talk privately. When they were alone, Nick asked the question.

"What happened to Wanda?"

"That, my friend, is a long story," Black said and then he answered Nick's question.

While Black talked to Nick about Wanda, Travis went to Flip's looking for Jackie. He'd told Travis that Jackie was operating out of Conversations. When Travis left to go to Conversations, Jada arrived at the game.

Everything and everybody stopped as Jada was escorted into the spot, as always, by Victor. Back's straightened when Zacaria and Chloe, along with two new ladies, Marisa Alvarez and Requia Blanchard, came in behind Jada.

Victor approached Flip and introduced him to Jada. "Good evening, Flip. It is a pleasure to finally meet you," Jada began graciously. "Victor has told me so much about you."

"Let's talk in the office, Flip," Victor suggested.

"Splendid." Jada looped her arm in Flip's. "Shall we?" Flip puffed up his chest, as men usually did when Jada walked beside them, and he escorted Jada into the office.

On the way, Jada was sure to make eye contact with Sonny Edwards. He nodded his head to acknowledge her and immediately became the subject of discussion at the card table.

Once they were in the office, Flip offered Jada and her ladies a seat. "Please have a seat."

"Thank you, Flip," Jada said and sat down. All four of her ladies stood behind her.

Flip looked at the beautiful ladies. "How are you ladies doing?" he asked, but none of them spoke a word until Jada nodded her head, giving them permission to speak to Flip.

"We're doing fine, sir," they all said in unison, and Flip couldn't help but be amused.

"How are you this evening?" Zacaria said and looked at Jada for approval.

Jada nodded her head. She was quite impressed with Zacaria; she was the total package. Zacaria was very pretty and had a body that could stop traffic. But to Jada, she was so much more. Zacaria was intelligent, aggressive, and she was determined to take the lead in everything she did. She had a very pleasing personality that would have every man gathered around her. And like Jada, Zacaria was resolute in her commitment to never be broke again.

"Is Mr. Black or Ms. Washington here this evening?"

"No, neither of them are here this evening."

"Unfortunate. I promised Mr. Black that I would deliver these lovely ladies."

"I'm sure that it will be all right if you leave them with Flip, Ms. West," Victor said. "I'm sure Flip will be able to explain how things work here and get them started."

"I will do nothing of the sort." Jada looked at Flip. "I am confident that you are quite capable of seeing that the ladies are properly oriented, Flip." Jada flashed her smile. "However, if it is acceptable to you, I will remain with the ladies to ensure that your way of doing things is in line with the way I have taught them."

Flip smiled and looked at Victor. "Yes, Ms. West, I think that is acceptable."

Victor glanced at Jada and then dropped his head, because he knew that it was only a matter of time before Jada had Flip and every other man in the spot, eating out of her hand.

32

At the same time that Jada was establishing herself at the game, Jackie was about to have visitors at Conversations. Angel and Avonte came in Conversations and had a seat at the bar.

"Do you see her?" Angel asked.

"I don't see her anywhere," Avonte replied.

Angel was wearing a Fendi outfit, consisting of a cashmere stripe top, bonded leather skirt, and chameleon metallic leather and satin pumps. While Avonte was looking dazzling in her boat neck, long sleeve Aidan Mattox dress with allover beaded embroidery, and a low V back.

Since she was Leon's younger sister, Angel had hung around Black's organization for years. When Leon moved his business to Jacksonville, she stayed in the city, and Black agreed to look out for her. Angel had met Avonte a few years earlier when she had become involved with two people that were on the wrong path. But when it was over, meaning Black made all her problems go away, Avonte was set for life.

After she graduated college, Avonte married Tyrone Petrocelli, who was in line to inherit his father's interest in the shipping business. After his untimely death, Avonte hooked up with Angel. She could tell early on that Avonte liked to be dominated. Angel knew that she was the one to do it, and do it without dogging Avonte in the process.

"You've had enough of that," Angel told Avonte when they got together.

The playful pair had spent the last year and a half traveling the world and seeing just how much fun they could have. Now they were back in the city and looking for something to get into.

They had been there for over an hour when Avonte noticed that Jackie had come in to the club with Spence. "There she is, Angel."

Angel turned quickly. "She's looking good, too."

That night, Jackie was dressed in Gucci from head to toe. A silk satin Georgette Raglan trench, Viscose V-neck tank, stretch wool holiday pants, and Claudie patent leather platform sandals. When Jackie saw them waving to her, she told Spence that she would get with him later and she went to the bar.

"Hello, ladies. I see you made it back to my spot," Jackie began.

Angel stood up and got close to Jackie. "Yes, we came back to see you."

"Really?"

"Yes, really."

"Why you two ladies wanna see me?" Jackie asked.

Angel took another step closer. "I'm a very good judge of character and I can tell just by looking at you that we will all get along great together."

Jackie laughed. "Do you really?"

"Yes. I really do."

"Why don't you show us around your spot, captain?" Avonte asked.

"What makes you think I'm a captain?"

"Mike told us," Angel said, and from that, Jackie knew that Angel was close to Black. But that made sense since she was Leon's sister and he and Black were very close.

"Sure," Jackie said. "Follow me."

After walking around the dance club, Jackie led Angel and Avonte to the stairs that led to the more exclusive areas of Conversations. She showed them the gambling room and then they went upstairs to the private rooms.

"This is where the women take their clients," Jackie said as they entered the third floor. "Looks like all the rooms are in use right now, but come on and I'll show you where they dance."

Jackie led Angel and Avonte into a small room that had only a couch and a pole. Avonte entered the room and slid her hand up and down the pole.

"So the women entertain their men in here?"

"Yup." Jackie sat down on the couch and Angel sat down next to her.

"Dance for the captain, Avonte," Angel said, and Avonte put her hand on the pole and began to dance.

"You look nice tonight," Jackie said to Avonte as she danced.

"You should see her without that dress. Avonte is fine as hell."

"Is she really?"

"Show her," Angel commanded, and Avonte began to slide her Aidan Mattox dress off her shoulders when Jackie felt the vibration of her phone. She looked at the screen and saw that she was receiving a text.

Jackie smiled and stood up. "I hate to break up this little party, but I gotta go."

"I understand," Angel said as Jackie left the room.

When she made it back down to the dance club, she saw Travis standing at the bar. Jackie rushed up to him and hugged her oldest friend. "Welcome back to the world, Travis."

"How're you doing, Jackie?"

"I'm doing great. What about you? How is island life treating you?"

"Barbados is wonderful."

"Come on," Jackie said and looped her arm in his. "Go with me to my office. Then you can tell me all about what you've been doing."

As they headed for her office, Jackie and Travis passed by Angel and Avonte. Angel nodded her head as they passed. "Friends of yours?" Travis asked.

"They trying to be my friends."

Travis looked at Angel and then at Avonte; she blew him a kiss and waved. "I wish they'd try and be my friends."

Jackie laughed. "Maybe we can arrange that; after I've tried them out first. Wouldn't want to present you with anything that wasn't up to your standards," Jackie said. She walked Travis by the bar and passed right by Agent McCullough.

33

After giving Travis the same tour of Conversations that she had just given Angel and Avonte, Jackie took Travis to her office. "Nice." Travis sat down and Jackie made them both a drink.

"So, tell me what you've been up to in Barbados?"

"Barbados is great, but that's not where I've been."

"Where you been?"

"Sana'a, Yemen with Nick and them."

"I thought the team was disbanded?"

"I thought so, too, until Colonel Mathis showed up in my living room one morning." Travis laughed. "Scared Trish half to death when she walked in the kitchen naked, and the Colonel said good morning."

"Who's Trish?"

"Friend of mine."

"Must be more than a friend if she was in your kitchen naked in the morning?"

"Okay, so we're more than friends."

"How much more?" Jackie asked, and felt a twinge of jealousy. Jackie had to laugh because she hadn't felt that way since she asked Freeze to kill Me'shelle Lawrence because she'd broken Travis's heart. Despite her tastes, she had always thought of Travis as being hers. Jackie loved Travis. Her mother still asked her when she and Travis were getting married.

"I don't know, Jackie. This might be the one."

"If it is, I'm happy for you," Jackie said and thought about *giving this Trish bitch, whoever the fuck she is, a dirt nap.*

Then Jackie sat and listened to Travis talk about his life in Barbados with Trish.

"There's a beach called Bath in St. John. It's one of the most popular beaches on the east coast of the island, because there are rarely strong currents there. Trish said that when she was a kid, her parents used to take them there on picnics. She took me walking there one day and remembered going up this hill where she found a very beautiful waterfall, but they couldn't tell where the water was coming from."

"Did you find it?" Jackie asked as if she really cared.

"No, she said she didn't know if it was still there or if it had dried up," Travis said and thought back to the walks they used to take to the north where they found a small waterfall and the remains of the old train line that once ran from Bridgetown to Bathsheba.

"So y'all had another mission," Jackie said, and Travis told her about the mission in Yemen. She wasn't pleased to find that she had been replaced on the team, but she understood.

"I know you're ready to put all that army shit behind you and get back to Barbados."

"Barbados has an army," Travis defended.

"Get the fuck outta here." Jackie laughed.

"It's the Barbados Defense Force. They're located off Bay Street in St. Michael. Trish told me that when she was a little girl, her dad used to take her to a beach behind their barracks. It's called Drill Hall."

"You been there?"

"Yeah, Trish took me there. The tide there was really, really low." Travis smiled. "She said that growing up; it felt like she could walk all the way out to where the waters are deep blue."

"Sounds like you're really enjoying life down there."

"You should've come with me."

"It's not like you didn't ask me to come," Jackie said and thought for a second or two about whether or not she regretted that decision.

"Sometimes I miss all of this. Being a part of the action," Travis began. "I think that was the main reason I didn't throw the colonel out." He laughed. "You know we had a ball in Yemen."

"I know you did."

"But then I think about my life now. I appreciate the little things," Travis paused, "like hanging out with Trish at Oistins on Friday night's."

"What's that?"

"By day it's a fish market and by night the shops and stalls are open. You can get all kinds of fish and chips—grilled, fried, boiled, baked—anyway you want," Travis said excitedly, "And there's music. All kinds of music. People hang out, drink, listen to the music, and dance. It's just a simpler life." Travis laughed. "Y'all must have really fucked up to get Black off that island."

"We did." Jackie told Travis what had gone on during Wanda's reign and how it led them to where they are now.

"What happened to Wanda?"

"Those that know what happened ain't saying."

"You think they killed her?"

"I don't know, and it is the shit nobody talks about; especially, around Black and Bobby."

"Good to know."

Jackie stood up. "So, since you missed all this, you feel like ridin' with me while I take care of something for Sherman?"

Travis laughed a little. "Sure, why not." He stood up.

"You armed?"

"No. I wasn't planning on doing any killing tonight."

Jackie laughed. "Then you shouldn't have come around us. 'Cause I swear, Travis, these last few weeks, all we been doing is killing." Jackie got up and opened her safe, and Travis armed himself as Spence came in the room.

"What's up, Travis?"

"It's all good, Spence. What's up with you?"

"I've been better," Spence said, thinking that things would be better if Carolina Royce would speak to him. But he did shoot her man in the back of the head, so what did he expect.

"Travis is gonna ride with us to do that thing for Sherman."

"Good. We were going to need some extra hands on this."

"What's the job?" Travis asked.

"Nothing major. I'll explain on the way," Jackie said. "Let's go."

34

It wasn't too much longer after that when Travis parked his car in front of Sweet Nectar; the club owned by Rob Berry. He got out of his car and walked over to the cars that were parked in front of the club. As quickly as he could, Travis dropped down and placed an explosive device under the car. When he was finished, Travis went back to his car, took out his cell phone, and dialed the number to Jackie's burner phone.

"I'm in position outside the club," Travis said.

"This is just like old times," Jackie said.

"I could ask the colonel to bump Carla and let you back on the team."

"I don't think so. I'm cool just where I am," Jackie said. In a way, she did miss the excitement. But when she really sat and thought about it, Jackie understood that she had all the excitement that she could handle right there. She started up the car.

"You ready, Spence?"

"Let's do it," he said and readied his AK47.

"Here we come, Travis."

"I'm ready."

As Travis picked up the Sony video camera, Jackie dropped the car in drive and sped off toward Sweet Nectar. Travis began shooting images of the five men standing in front of the club. As Jackie drove by Sweet Nectar, Spence opened fire, and the men dove for the ground. One of Berry's men got up and tried to get a shot off, but that wasn't happening because of the gunfire. Two of the other men opened fire, but both men quickly dropped to the ground when Jackie stopped the car and joined Spence in firing at the building.

The men fired at Jackie and Spence until their guns were empty. When the front door swung open and more of Berry's men came running out of the club, Jackie got back in the car and drove off. As Berry's men moved into the street to shoot at the car and give chase, Travis pressed the button on the detonator and blew up the car. That not only stopped them from chasing Jackie and Spence, but took down a few of Berry's men in the process.

Travis started up his car and drove away knowing that he had gotten Sherman exactly what he wanted. Now they knew what type of force they would encounter if they tried to take Rob Berry at Sweet Nectar.

In another part of the city, armed with one of her favorite weapons, the SIG 556 autoloading rifle which fired 223 caliber shells from its 30-shot detachable box magazine, Monika took out her binoculars and watched the house. She was positioned on the roof across the street from her target. Now Monika waited patiently for Terentius Sancho to come into the room.

Monika aimed the sight on the weapon to hit her target dead-on at three-hundred yards. She checked to determine the proper windage needed for a 10 mph crosswind. When Sancho came in the room, Monika took aim and fired at her target. He went down from a clean shot to the head. With her mission completed, Monika packed up her rifle.

It was after midnight when two men came out of a house in South Hampton and walked by the tree where Nick was positioned. From that position, Nick knew how often Narez's men swept the grounds and in what time intervals.

He knew the location and angle of the security cameras and where the blind spots were.

Once the men passed his position, Nick put on his night vision goggles and made his move. He jumped down from the tree he'd been watching from and made his way to the wall. Confident that he had not been detected, Nick removed his backpack and took out a rope with a grappling hook attached to it, and preceded to repel the wall.

Now that Nick was on the grounds, he checked his position against the angle of the camera's before moving toward the house. He stayed low to the ground and began his approach to the house. Once Nick made it to the house, he entered through the back door

As he expected, the ground floor was empty. Nick moved quickly and carefully toward the steps and went up to the second level. He could hear them talking as he approached the study. Ambrosius Faustinus and Alano Narez were startled when Nick entered the room with his Beretta raised. Before either man could react, Nick fired at Faustinus and shot him twice in the head. Then he turned his weapon on Narez and fired twice. Both shots hit him in the head and the impact put Narez down. Then Nick walked up to them and shot each man in the chest. With both targets eliminated, Nick left the scene.

Greg Milson had just rolled over on his side when he heard the footsteps of the guard approaching. Then he stopped and made the announcement. "Get up, Milson. You're outta here."

Since he thought that the guard must be talking to the inmate in the cell next to his, Milson didn't move. He closed his eyes, yawned, and tried to go back to sleep.

"Milson!" the guard yelled this time. "I said get up, you're outta here."

Milson lifted his head. "What are you talking about, officer?"

"About you getting your sorry ass outta here." The guard unlocked his cell.

"There must be some mistake. Ain't no way in hell I'm supposed to be getting out of here. I'm in protective custody."

Milson was there to testify that he witnessed Detective Kirkland murder Donaldo Baker. So he spent twenty-three hours alone in his small cell and only came out for an hour a day for a shower and recreation. There were no letters, no visitors, and no contact with the world.

"Maybe they're here to move your worthless ass some place safer. I don't know and I don't care. Just get your shit and come on."

Since that explanation made sense, Milson got up and followed the guard off the cell block. He was taken to a holding cell and waited while he was processed out and released to the custody of two detectives. They drove Milson across the George Washington Bridge to an Econo Lodge on

Hudson Terrace, in Fort Lee, New Jersey. Once Milson had made himself comfortable in the room, the detectives got up and opened the door. Rain and Smoke walked in. She handed each of them an envelope.

"Thanks, Cavanaugh. We'll take it from here," Rain said, and Detective Cavanaugh and his partner left the room.

"What's this shit about?" Milson muttered.

Smoke rushed at Milson and snatched him off of the bed.

"You wanna be a fuckin' witness?" Rain asked.

Smoke dragged Milson in front of the mirror. While Smoke held him up, Rain put the barrel of her gun to his temple.

"Witness this," she said and pulled the trigger.

After a three hour and forty-five minute flight, Black and Shy, along with Napoleon, arrived aboard a charter at Luis Munoz Marin International Airport in San Juan, Puerto Rico. Once he passed through customs and had collected their luggage, Napoleon saw a limousine driver with a sign that said BLACK. When their driver had secured their luggage, he took them to the St. Regis Bahia Beach Resort.

"How far is Luquillo?" Black asked as they drove to the resort.

"About fifty kilometers. So, if you stay on the coastal highway going east from San Juan, you'll reach Luquillo Beach. It is one of the most popular and nicest public beaches in the world."

The St. Regis Bahia Beach Resort invites their guests to embrace the romantic setting of a Caribbean coconut plantation nestled between a lush national forest and the sparkling sea. Once they were checked in and had seen their rooms, Black called the contact name he was given. He was told to relax and enjoy the island.

"You will be contacted soon."

After that, both Shy and Napoleon announced that they were hungry, so they went to a place called Barbakoa.

"¿Está preparado para realizar el pedido?"

"No habla mucho español," Shy said.

"Are you folks ready to order?"

Since Shy was the only one that could speak a little Spanish, she looked at the menu. "What is Yuquiyú?"

"Yuquiyú is a perfectly seasoned angus beef filet with your choice of shrimp or salmon."

"I'll have that with salmon," Black said.

"And Cacimar; what is that?"

"Cacimar is shrimp sauteed Barbakoa style."

"And the Jumacao?"

"Jumacao is a combination platter with chicken wings, spare ribs, grilled sausage, and mofonguitos yucca."

"I'll have that and make it a large please, sir," Napoleon said.

"And I will have the Cacimar," Shy said.

After dinner, Shy convinced Black to go on a sunset sail cruise, but it wasn't easy. The evening began with them leisurely sailing on a private catamaran around Fajardo Bay. That night they relaxed; took in the balmy breezes of the tropics while they watched the Caribbean sunset.

Shy looked at Black, and for just a moment, she could see his vulnerability. That bothered her, because Mike Black was the strongest person she had ever met. Shy moved a little closer to her husband and slid her hand across his chest, admiring the contours of it before leaning in running her tongue around his ear lobe. They were interrupted when a member of the crew served them rum punch and hors d'oeuvres. Napoleon shook his head.

After the cruise, Black and Shy returned to their limousine. Napoleon opened the door for them, and then he got in the front seat with the driver. As soon as they drove off and headed back to the resort, Shy got back to what she was doing.

She unbuttoned his shirt and began licking and sucking his nipple until it grew hard under her tongue, and she continued until he moaned. Black gently pulled her face up to his and kissed her deeply while he stared into her eyes. Shy was hungry for Black and wanted to feel him inside of her. She was already wet and had been that way all day. Black kissed Shy tenderly and to her it felt like his tongue was dancing with hers. He pulled up the Etro asymmetrical dress that Shy was wearing; his fingers blazed a trail up her thighs that made her skin tingle. There were no words that could describe the sensation that Shy felt when Black started to rub her swollen clit. Her body began to quiver just as they stopped in front of the hotel.

Their evening ended with a romantic walk on the beach. "As romantic as it can be with Napoleon following us," Shy said. "But we'll be alone soon and then you'll be all mine."

When they made it to their room, Black went out on the balcony and sat down on the chaise lounge with Shy following him. She let her dress trail down her body and pool at her feet before stepping out and sitting next to him. She removed his shirt and then she kissed him with as much love and passion as she could muster. With Shy's help, Black got out of his pants and their kissing resumed. Her head drifted back as the circling of his finger was driving her insane.

Black entered Shy in one thrust and began moving slowly in and out of her as she arched her back in anxious anticipation of each stroke. In that moment, Shy felt filled with his love and wanted nothing more than to satisfy his every desire. Black showed her so much love, and Shy felt deep in her soul that no other woman could ever know the feeling she was feeling right then.

Suddenly, Black flipped Shy over so she was on top of him. She planted her feet at his sides, braced her hands on his thighs, and arched her back to take all of him in. He grabbed Shy's ass and she rode him harder, faster. With her eyes squeezed tightly shut, Shy grinded her hips in circles and then up and down until Black was so deep inside her that her body started to tremble from the exquisite sweet pain. It felt so good to have him so deep, hitting her spot.

He took a nipple into his mouth, sucking on it hard, making her muscles tighten around him, bringing her closer to climax. Shy grabbed the back of his head and held him there before he rolled her on her back. Black eased himself inside her and she wrapped her legs around his waist. She felt that tingling sensation dancing in the balls of her feet. Shy worked her hips and inner muscles while licking his nipples. His body began to tremble and Shy rocked her hips furiously. Black's entire body went rigid and he exploded inside her.

"I love you, Cassandra. More than words could ever express."

"I love you, too."

The next morning after breakfast, Black hoped that they would be contacted, but when that didn't happen, Shy began making plans for the rest of the day.

"I know," Shy began, knowing what he'd say. "We could go to JungleQui Rainforest Ecoadventure Park."

"That ain't happening." Black rolled over and looked at Shy. "I got a better idea."

"I'm listening."

"We could go to San Juan and walk around old town and get into whatever."

154

"I like that idea. But I do want to go to the San Juan National Historic Site and the Castillo de San Cristobal."

"I'm really not feeling the Castillo de San Cristobal."

"Why not?" Shy asked, and then she thought about it. "Oh yeah, it was a man named Cristobal that shot you. San Juan National Historic Site it is then," she said quickly and smiled at Black, knowing that they were the same place.

"Deal."

The attractions of Old San Juan were within walking distance of each other, but they decided to take the trolley. "It goes all through the area and you can get off wherever. The trolley tends to stay very full on afternoons when cruise ships are in," a woman cautioned as they waited for the trolley.

"We'll be all right. Can't be any worse than the train in New York at rush hour," Shy said.

"When was the last time you rode the train?" Black asked.

"I'm just saying."

While they rode the trolley, Shy noticed the large number of architecturally similar buildings that lined each street. Then they got to La Perla, a tiny oceanside neighborhood over the north wall and Norzagaray Street.

"Breathtaking views of the Atlantic Ocean can be seen from the tunnel entrance of the El Morro Fort Lawn Cemetery. The guide book says it's not advisable to enter La Perla either on foot or in a vehicle," Shy said.

"Why is that?"

"It is known for a high rate of illegal activities, and there is no police presence there."

"My kind of place."

That night, Black and Shy went dancing at Club Lazer, a tri-level dance club with a rooftop terrace. The following day they spent the day at the beach and had dinner at Santaella. *Shy loved the Lobster macaroni and cheese.* That evening was spent at Parguera Blues Café, a jazz and blues venue, and danced the night away at Stargate.

"I'm ready for the vacation to be over and get this meeting over with," Black said.

"Relax and enjoy yourself, Michael," Shy said and rested her head on his chest. But it was hard for Black when there was a war going on in the city.

The next morning, their driver came and knocked on their door. He invited Black and Shy for coffee.

"Good coffee. Very important you come."

"About time," Black said.

They were taken to La Familia Bakery 2 on Urb Rio Grande Estates Calle. When they walked in the bakery, the first person they saw was Hector Villanueva.

Both Black and Shy had history with Hector. Years ago, when Shy was an entrepreneur and her sources had dried up, she made a deal to buy product from Hector. Black, on the other hand, fucked Hector's wife, Nina. When Black told Shy about the invitation, she was apprehensive at first.

"So, what you're telling me is that you want me, your wife, to sit up in another one of your ex's faces? Is that what you're telling me, Michael?"

"Yes."

Shy shook her head. "Next thing you know, Regina will come out the woodwork," Shy said, joking about the woman that Black once had a relationship with.

Black looked at Shy. "I wouldn't be surprised if she didn't come to RJ's sixteenth birthday party."

Shy smiled a devilish smile.

"What are you smiling about?"

"It might be interesting to meet her; or should I say, for her to meet me."

"Why?"

"Because she was desperate to marry you, and I'm Mrs. Mike Black."

As Hector looked on, Black and Shy stood at the door to La Familia Bakery 2, while Napoleon had a look around. Once he was satisfied that it was safe for them to enter, he nodded at Black and they came in.

Hector stood up to greet them. "Black," he said and shook Black's hand before turning his attention to Shy. "And beautiful Shy." Hector bowed and kissed Shy's hand. "Nobody was happier than me to hear that you were still alive and had survived your ordeal."

"Thank you for saying so, Hector. I am glad to be here. Thank you very much for inviting us. From what we've seen of it, this is a beautiful island."

"Thank you. Please—have a seat." They sat down at the table with Hector and he took a sip of his espresso. "Can I offer you anything? Some espresso, perhaps?" He smiled. "You know, a good espresso will depend on what coffee beans you use."

"Is that a fact?"

"Yes. You see, there should be bitterness, but not too much, sourness in balance with the bitterness, a bit of sweetness, good body and an aroma." Hector raised his cup. "Yaucono is the best coffee in Puerto Rico."

Black and Shy had espresso and shared a cream horn with dark chocolate topping, filled with a combination of whip cream and Bavarian cream. While Napoleon enjoyed a delicious breakfast of scrambled eggs, ham, Swiss cheese, tomatoes and lettuce.

They made small talk over breakfast. Once breakfast was over, Hector invited Black and Shy to ride with him to Luquillo, which was located east of Rio Grande on the northeast coast. That was where Hector was born and raised.

Hector walked out of the bakery and stepped up to a Ferrari 458 Spider. "Get in."

"But this is a two-seater," Shy pointed out.

Hector smiled. "I am sure that this won't be the first time you sat on his lap," he said and got in the car.

"Why can't we just take the limo," Shy pointed at the limo as it drove off. Shy looked at Black; he got in the Ferrari.

Once they were in, Napoleon closed the car door. "I'll get a cab and come behind you, Boss."

Hector drove away fast and Napoleon rushed off to find a cab. He drove out Interstate PR3 from Rio Grande to Luquillo.

"Luquillo was founded in 1797 and is known as La Capital del Sol."

"Sun capital," Shy said.

"¿Hablas español?"

"I barely passed high school Spanish, so I catch a word or two here and there."

"The town was named after the Indian cacique Luquillo, who died a few years after the last Indian rebellion in 1513."

After Hector drove them around the area where he grew up, he took them to the beaches in Luquillo. First he took them to Playa Azul. "This would be my second favorite beach in Luquillo."

"What's your favorite?" Shy asked.

"Playa La Pared it is the next beach heading east. The beach runs alongside the road and is separated from the road by a wall."

"That how the beach got its name?" Shy asked.

"In fact it is. The Wall Beach."

As they walked back to the Ferrari, Napoleon finally found them. To which, Hector said, "Your man is good."

Napoleon followed in the cab, while Hector drove Black and Shy to his home, a beach front property in Palma Sola, Canovanas. The property was a picture of tranquility and peace; a perfect view of the Atlantic Ocean.

"This is beautiful, Hector," Shy said as they walked out from the balcony to the beach.

"It is ideal for meditation and reflection," Hector said.

They had a seat on the balcony and Hector's butler came with drinks. He poured a glass of Don Q Gran Añejo for Shy and Hector, and Rémy Martin XO for Black.

"I hope I got the drinks right. I remember you being a rum drinker, Shy."

"This is perfect. In fact, this is what I drink."

Later in the day, the cook prepared a feast of Puerto Rican delicacies. Classic Puerto Rican black beans and rice, barbecued, fish stew, Pork a La Criolla, sweet corn bread muffins, Arroz Con Gandules, which is brown rice and pigeon peas. And for dessert, there was Mrs. Pischke's Rum Cake and plenty of island piña colada to drink with their meal.

Just as they were about to sit down for dinner Hector's wife, Nina, made her first appearance of the day. It was a meal that she could have very easily skipped. Because of her feelings for and her past relationship with Black, she wasn't looking forward to spending an evening with Shy.

Both Hector and Black stood up when she came into the room. Shy rolled her eyes. "Good evening everybody. I hope I didn't keep you all waiting for very long."

"Not at all," Hector said and turned to Shy. "Shy, may I introduce you to my wife, Nianza."

"It's a pleasure to finally meet you, Nianza." Shy smiled. "Michael has told me so much about you," she said, and Nina cringed at the thought of it.

After the meal was concluded, Nina excused herself. Black, Shy, and Hector went out on the balcony for coffee. "I want to thank you for your hospitality. The food was excellent," Shy said.

Hector patted his stomach. "That is why I have gained weight since I've been here."

"Why are you here, Hector?" Black asked.

"What, do you think that you are the only one that can run his business from the Caribbean?"

"I meant no disrespect."

"None taken, my friend. The truth is that my mother is sick. She's dying. I will be here until the Holy Mother calls her home."

"I understand," Black said.

"I'm so sorry to hear that, Hector," Shy added.

As the evening wore on, Shy excused herself. Even though Shy had done business with Hector before, she knew that Hector would be uncomfortable and somewhat reluctant to talk business in front of a woman. After Shy was gone, Hector and Black talked.

"Normally, I would ask what I can do for you, but I already know. Nado Benitez and his people, and the war you started with them," Hector paused. "Or should I say that Wanda started."

"Yes," Black said softly and thought about the pain Wanda and her betrayal had caused him. "You always seem to know everything."

"It only seems that way." Hector laughed. "Now, please tell me what I can do to help you, my friend."

Over coffee, Black laid out for Hector the situation with Benitez. Then he explained what he wanted from Hector and how it would work out.

"At this point Benitez, Balendin, Sancho, Faustinus, and Narez are dead. My people tell me that they are in disarray. You move in now; take back what once belonged to your family."

"I think we can do business."

Now that his business with Hector was completed, Black was ready to get back to the city, but Shy had other plans. She insisted that they stay another couple of days before they went back to the city.

"Unfortunately, the war will still be going on when you get back."

Meanwhile, back in New York, Rain was sitting alone in her office at J.R.'s, when she got a call from Cal Worrell, her informant in Brill's organization.

"What's up, Cal?"

"You still want Brill?"

"You know I do."

"You can catch him right now."

"Where he at?"

"Do you know Bria Bryan?"

"His other, other woman; yeah, I know that ho."

"He's there now and he's only got one man with him."

"Good looking out, Cal. Thanks."

Rain hung up the phone and put on her vest. Then she grabbed her guns and left J.R.'s. Her better judgment told her that she shouldn't go alone. But at the same time, fueled by her anger and rage, Rain wasn't thinking clearly.

When she got to the apartment building where Bria Bryan lived, Rain sat in her car for a half hour and checked out the scene. Once she was confident that things were as Cal said, Rain got out of the car and walked toward the building.

As soon as Rain got to the steps, four of Brill's men came rushing out and began firing at her.

"Shit!" Rain yelled as she took out her guns, stopped and turned around quickly. Rain fired a couple of shots at them as they came down the steps. That gave her enough time to make it to her car. Rain emptied her clip and got in. She looked in her rearview mirror and saw that Brill's men had made it to their car. Rain reloaded her gun as she weaved through traffic. Brill's men started shooting.

Rain took a sharp turn onto Allerton Avenue as Brill's men continued their pursuit. When she crossed Holland Avenue the light turned red and Rain floored it. She made it through the light, but so did Brill's men. They had to swerve to avoid the oncoming cars, but they kept coming. When Rain passed the train station and approached the Bronx River Parkway, she knew what she was going to do.

Just then, Rain cut across the lanes and continued onto the on ramp, causing the cars to crash in front of Brill's men. They slammed on their brakes, turned sharply, and followed Rain onto the Parkway. As she moved through traffic, Brill's men kept firing at Rain's car and blew out her back window. Rain stayed low and kept driving as she approached an exit on the parkway. But she took the turn too fast; her car went into a spin and slammed into a guard rail. When Brill's men got there, Rain got out of the car. She opened fire with both guns and then took off running.

Brill's men ran after her, firing shots all the way. Rain stopped and fired. They took cover behind a car and shot back. She ran down the street until she reached the next corner. Rain dropped down behind a car and stayed still and quiet.

It was then that she remembered something that Nick had told her. "Sometimes when you're being hunted by superior numbers, you gotta turn things around. You become the hunter."

Rain watched through the car window as four of Brill's men stopped at the corner. They stood and talked before they split up. She watched which direction the men went in. When the last man left the corner, Rain stood up and followed as he went down the street looking for her. When she had a clear shot, Rain fired at him.

One of Brill's men heard the shot and ran back down the street. Rain was standing in the shadows as he ran past her. She took aim and fired; her shot hit him in the back. Rain walked up to him and shot him twice more.

When Rain saw two men running down the street, she took off running. Rain stopped, turned, and fired with both guns before she ran in a building. Rain hid and watched as the last two men came in the building. As they split up again, Rain went after one of them. When she watched the man go in a room, Rain went in after him. She came through the door blasting shots and the man went down.

Now there was just one of Brill's men left.

Rain moved through the building and then she saw him going up some steps. When he reached the top of the stairs, Rain went up after him. She watched as he walked through the floor looking for her. He went in a room and looked around. When he saw that she wasn't hiding in there, Brill's man turned around; and there was Rain with both of her guns pointed at him.

"Looking for me?"

Rain let go with both guns.

Later that night, Rain arrived at the door to Cal Worrell's apartment. When she found the door opened,

Rain knew that it wasn't good. She took out her guns and entered the apartment. It didn't take her long to find Cal seated at the kitchen table with his cell in front of him, and a bullet in the back of his head.

When they got back from Puerto Rico, Scarlett invited Black and Shy to dinner at her apartment to meet her family. Shy was skeptical about the whole sister thing, so while they were in Puerto Rico, Shy insisted that Black have Bobby check her out. To accomplish his mission, Bobby went to see Gladys at Big Night Records. "Mike needs to know if this woman is really his sister."

"Trust me, Mr. Ray, I understand his need to know."

Bobby smiled at Gladys. "Please, call me Bobby."

Gladys smiled at Bobby. "Bobby it is."

The following day, Gladys called Scarlett and asked her to stop by the office for a chat. "Can I offer you something to drink, Scarlett?"

"Just some water, thank you," she said politely, and that was enough DNA to get tested.

Once it was established that Scarlett was indeed his sister, Shy was ready to welcome her into the family. When they arrived, Black introduced Shy. "Cassandra, this is my sister, Scarlett."

"It's a pleasure to meet you, Cassandra."

"Please call me Shy."

Scarlett laughed a little. "Why Shy?"

"Long story."

After that, Scarlett asked them to make themselves comfortable while she got her children. "This is my daughter, Sherraine, and my son, Gordy. Children, this is your Uncle Mike and your Aunt Shy," Scarlett said.

Once introductions were done, Scarlett sent the children back to their room so she could finish getting dinner ready to serve.

"You need help with anything?" Shy asked and Black laughed a little. Shy nudged him.

"No, everything is just 'bout done."

"Just let me know," Shy said and gave Black the evil eye.

"I was hoping to meet your children as well," Scarlett said from the kitchen.

"Our children are in Freeport visiting Michael's mother," Shy said, and Black nodded in approval of her answer.

Scarlett served her family a delicious dinner of stewed beef, rice and peas, curry cabbage, breadfruit salad, oxtail stew, and homemade coconut mango ice cream with coconut mango cookies for dessert. After dinner, Scarlett gave the kids some chocolate milk and put them to bed for the night.

"Now, let's have some big people lemonade," she said, and Shy was intrigued.

"What is big people lemonade?"

"Three lemons, three limes, four oranges, five cups of water, and a cup of rum. Back in St. Vincent, my family home is surrounded by citrus trees. Oranges, grapefruit, shaddock, limes, and lemons. Basically, we were never out of freshly made juice with our meals."

As they sipped big people lemonade, Scarlett told her new family her story. Convinced that she had to go to New York to get her music career started, Scarlett left St. Vincent against her family's wishes.

"You don't need to go to New York just to sing, Scarlett," her mother said. "You can stay right here."

"And do what? Keep singing in church? I want more than that," a nineteen-year-old Scarlett said.

"You're breaking your mother's heart, Scarlett. Can't you see that?" her father Fenton asked.

"Can't you both see what not following my dream is doing to me?"

Never wanting to deny his baby girl anything, her father gave her the money. Scarlett hugged her father. "Thank you, Daddy."

"You just be careful up there and make us all proud," Fenton told his daughter.

Scarlett caught the first flight to New York City and her rude awakening began. It didn't take her long to realize that breaking into the music business was going to be harder than she thought. Scarlett was sure that once people heard her voice that the rest would be easy.

"What I found was a bunch of people who were simply out to take advantage of the little West Indian girl; fresh off the banana barge and dumber than a stump. After a while, my work visa had expired and I was nowhere near my goal."

In order to stay in the country, Scarlett paid a man who introduced her to Ellis. Scarlett married him and after a long and expensive process, Scarlett got her green card. However, the two began to like each other and the arranged marriage of convenience became a real marriage.

"And for a while we were very happy together. A few months later, I was pregnant with Sherraine and our relationship began falling apart," Scarlett said. It began the day Ellis put his hands on Scarlett. But she wasn't about to tell her new family that.

"What happened?" Shy asked.

"Ellis lost his job, money got tight; we started arguing."

"That's too bad," Shy said.

"Six months after having the baby, I was back in St Vincent without Ellis. But we kept in touch, you know, for the sake of the baby," Scarlett said with the use of air quotes.

"Isn't that how it always goes."

"When I got back to St. Vincent, Daddy got me a job as a waitress at the Buccament Bay Resort. That's where this new life began for me."

"How so?"

"I got my first break when a member of the house band happened to hear me singing one day. I joined the band, and soon I became its lead singer."

"Now that sounds like a dream come true," Shy said.

"It is."

"And you didn't have to leave St. Vincent to do it," Black said.

"Something my mother is quite fond of pointing out to me." Scarlett laughed.

With her life and career on the rise and his life and future circling the drain, Ellis saw his wife, Scarlett, as an opportunity. He promised to be a good husband and father to their daughter and begged Scarlett for a second chance.

"Please, Scarlett. All I need is a chance and I will show you that I have changed. The man I was before doesn't exist anymore."

"I want to believe you, Ellis; I really do. I'm just not sure."

I CAME TO BRING THE PAIN

At the time, Scarlett and her band were playing at the Ports of Call Resort in the Turks and Caicos Islands. After a lot of long contemplation, Scarlett decided to send Ellis a ticket to join her there.

"This is only a test run. We'll see how the next couple of weeks go and then we'll go on from there," Scarlett said.

"Thank you, Scarlett. You won't regret this, you'll see," Ellis told her.

When Ellis got to Turks and Caicos, he and Scarlett got along just fine. It was the way it was when they first met and got married. While Scarlett performed with the band, Ellis traveled with them until Scarlett got pregnant with Gordy.

After the birth of their second child, Scarlett and Ellis returned to St. Vincent until the band got a long-term engagement in Aruba to perform at the Yahnica Beach Resort and Spa. Ellis stayed on the island with their children and began working with Scarlett's family. While the band was performing in Aruba, Scarlett got Gladys's attention and she was signed.

"Is your husband coming?" Black asked. "I was looking forward to meeting him.'

"Oh, he called and said that he was tied up with something," Scarlett lied.

Ellis Brock was a native New Yorker and he was glad to be back in the city. On their first night back in the city, instead of going to Impressions with Scarlett, Ellis went to a bar looking for his childhood friend, Big Walt McDonald.

When he got there, Ellis took a seat at a table and it wasn't long before a waitress approached. "What can I get for you?"

"Double Crown on the rocks."

When the waitress returned with his drink, Ellis paid her and then told her why he was there. "I'm looking for Carolina Royce."

"You found her."

"I thought so."

"And who might you be?"

"My name is Ellis Brock. Walt used to talk about you all the time," Ellis told Carolina.

"Nice to meet you," Carolina said sadly and began to walk away.

"Where is Walt anyway?"

"You don't know?"

"Know what?"

"I'm sorry to be the one to have to tell you, but Walt is dead."

"Dead?" Ellis asked in total shock.

"Murdered."

"Who killed him?"

"Walt was killed by people that work for Mike Black."

"Mike Black?"

Carolina saw the look on his face. "You know him?"

"I'm married to his half sister," Ellis said.

"I think that you should talk to Lloyd Brill."

"Who's that?"

"Walt used to work for Brill. Brill is at war with Black and his people; that's how Walt got killed," Carolina explained. "But you being Mike Black's brother-in-law puts you in a unique position."

Ellis began to see how he could use the relationship and the situation to make some real money for himself. The following day, Carolina took Ellis and introduced him to Brill. "So you're Mike Black's brother-in-law, huh?"

"Yeah, but Walt was my boy. We came up together."

"You stick around," Brill said and got up. "We'll see if you can make yourself useful to me."

After that meeting, Mike Black's brother-in-law went to work for Lloyd Brill. Ellis was a good soldier and made himself very useful to his new boss.

Always looking for an advantage in his war with Mike Black, Brill figured that he finally had one. He immediately began thinking of ways that he could use Ellis. Then all of a sudden, it hit him like a shot.

"I know exactly what to do," Brill said and began planning the kidnapping of Scarlett Brock.

40

Armed with a new sketch of the killer that no one else had, Mitchell continued her search for a killer. Each night, Mitchell paid another visit to the bars in Chelsea that she had previously visited. Only difference was, this time Mitchell brought Carmen along with her.

"You and I are going after her, Carmen, and we are going to catch her."

"When we catch her, what are you going to do?"

"Let's just catch her first," Mitchell said.

Their first stop was Gallow Green on West 27th Street between Tenth and Eleventh Avenues. "I did a piece about this place while I was on restaurant review," Carmen said.

"I didn't get anything at all when I was here the first time." Mitchell laughed. "But that was the story just about everywhere I went. Very few had seen the victims and nobody saw anybody with them. I'm hoping the new sketch will turn things around."

At each stop the detective showed the sketch of the serial killer to the employees at each establishment. "Welcome back, Detective," Julie, the co-owner of the Flatiron Lounge said as she placed a Beijing Pitch in front of her.

"It's this drink. I can't seem to get enough of them." The detective laughed. "Julie, this is my friend—"

"Carmen Taylor!" Julie said excitedly and placed a bar napkin in front of Carmen. "It would be my honor to serve you a drink. What are you drinking?"

"You have got to try her signature drink," Mitchell insisted.

"What is your signature drink?"

"Beijing Pitch."

"What is that?"

"A drink made with jasmine-infused vodka and white peach puree," Julie said.

"No, I'm not big on vodka. Just bring me a Ron Zacapa XO on the rocks, please."

"Coming up."

When Julie returned with Carmen's drink, the detective showed her the new sketch artist rendition of the killer. "Have you seen this woman in here before?"

"You still working the same case, Detective?"

"I am."

Julie looked at the sketch. "You know," she paused, "I think I have seen her before."

Mitchell took out images of the victims. "Was she with any of these men?"

Once again, Julie looked at the images and shook her head. "Sorry, Detective, I don't remember seeing her with anybody. I think she's been here a few times, but she mostly sat by herself."

"Anybody talk to her, send her a drink, maybe?" Carmen asked.

"I seem to remember her being pretty good at dismissing guys that sat down next to her."

"And you never saw her leave with anybody?" Mitchell asked.

"Not that I remember."

As their search continued, Detective Mitchell and Carmen had been to The Half King, Raines Law Room, and The Rye House. After seeing the sketch, many of the people that they talked to were able identify the woman as having been there before, but not necessarily with any of the victims. Mitchell asked each of them to call her if the woman showed up again.

They were just getting ready to leave The Rye House when Mitchell noticed a man that she believed had been following them all evening. She had seen him at each of the bars that they'd visited that night. "Did you know that there is somebody following us, Carmen?"

Carmen smiled. "I don't know it for sure, but if there was somebody following me, I wouldn't be the least bit surprised," Carmen said.

"I'll be back, Carmen," Mitchell said and went to approach the man.

"Wait!" Carmen shouted over the music, but Mitchell kept going.

When Mitchell got to the spot where the man was standing, he was gone. Just then, Carmen caught up with the detective. "Where is he?"

"Gone." Mitchell looked at Carmen. "You know who it is; and he is following you, isn't he, Carmen?"

"I don't know for sure," Carmen began and told Mitchell just enough for her to understand what was happening, and then she told her what Jada had told her.

"You and your criminal friends." Mitchell shook her head. "I know that we have had this conversation before, so I won't go into it again."

"Thank you," Carmen rolled her eyes and said, relieved that Mitchell wasn't about to break into that lecture again.

"But, Carmen, I really need you to give serious thought to putting some more distance between yourself and these people."

"I hear you, Diane. I really do."

"But this shit I'm talking went in one ear and out the other."

"I wouldn't have put it quite that way, but yeah."

At Pierre Loti on West 15th Street, the story was the same. "Have you seen this woman in here before?"

"Yeah, I've seen her before."

"Was she with any of these men, or did you see her leave with anybody?"

The answer to that question was the same. "Never saw her with anybody?"

As she did at each stop, Mitchell asked them to call her if they saw the woman again. When they got ready to leave, they stopped and talked to the doorman. He was busy with customers when they came in. Mitchell flashed her badge. "I'm Detective Mitchell. Do you have a minute to look at some images?"

"Sure." The doorman looked at the sketch. "Yeah, I know her. She comes here all the time."

"You know her, or you've seen her before, which is it?" Mitchell asked.

"I know her," he said slow and reluctantly. "What's this about?"

"Just want to ask her some questions. How well do you know her?"

"Like I said, she's been here a few times, and one of those times we hooked up."

"You know her name and where she lives?"

"I don't know where she lives, but her name is Tyhedra Crawford."

It was just before midnight when Jackie, Travis, and Spence walked into The Blue Flame; a strip club owned by Rob Berry. They were there looking for Rex Ericson. He ran the club for Rob Berry and was his best friend.

"Anybody see him?" Jackie asked as she scanned the spot.

Both Travis and Spence smiled as they were momentarily captivated by the women who were dancing onstage.

"I don't see him," Spence said over the music. "But what I do see is quality."

"Serious quality," Travis added as they watched as two beautiful women dance together.

Jackie looked and saw what they were looking at. "Damn!" Jackie shook her head. "Now that really is quality."

Just then, two of Rex Ericson's men stepped in front of Jackie and got in her face. "Where the fuck you niggas think y'all goin'?"

Spence reached over Jackie's shoulder and put a gun in the man's face. "Any fuckin' where she pleases."

Another man stepped up, swung at Travis, and hit him in the face. Travis rolled with the punch, took out his gun and hit the man with it. The blow from the pistol busted open his face and soon he was covered with blood.

Jackie took out both of her guns, fired them both at the ceiling to get everybody's attention, and then she yelled. "I'm looking for Rex Ericson and I know you're in here, Rex. So stop acting like the pussy I know you are and come out."

Two more men came running out of the office with automatic weapons. They opened fire. Their customers dove for the floor as the two men stood in the open and sprayed the bar with bullets. Travis and Spence ran and returned fire as Jackie took cover. Once she found cover, Jackie began firing so Travis and Spence could get to better cover.

Jackie crawled along the floor until she could get a clear shot at the shooters. When one stopped to reload, Travis stood up and hit him with two shots to the chest. The man went down and Travis took cover as his partner began firing at him. When he turned to fire at Travis, Jackie shot him in the back of the head.

The man that Travis hit in the face got up from the floor and pulled his weapon. Before he could get off a shot, Travis raised his weapon and fire three shots into his chest. He went down again. Spence stood over him and put two in his head. Then Travis and Spence moved in on the remaining shooter. He kept firing until he was empty. He stood and put his hands up. Jackie walked up to him, raised her weapon, and shot him as she passed on her way to the office.

"I know your bitch-ass is in there, Rex. Might as well come out before we come in there and drag your bitch-ass out," Jackie said.

When Jackie nodded her head, Travis and Spence moved toward the office. Once they had positioned themselves on either side of the door, Travis hit the door hard and stepped back quickly. Rex began firing shots wildly through the door. When the shooting stopped, Travis and Spence stepped inside. Rex was crotched down behind his desk, trying to reload.

"What's up, Rex?" Jackie said.

Spence grabbed Rex and pulled him to his feet. "Ain't you glad to see me, Rex?" Then he and Travis dragged him out of the office. Jackie got in his face.

Travis punched him in the stomach and then pushed Rex toward Spence. He hit him twice in the face, and then slammed his face down on a table. He pushed Rex and he stumbled and fell over a table. As Rex tried to get to his feet, Travis picked him up.

When they left The Flame, Jackie, with a gun in each hand, led the way out as Travis held on to Rex Ericson and Spence pointed a gun at his temple.

They drove Rex back to Conversations and took him in the back door, and then they went upstairs to the office. When they arrived in her office, Jackie laid a drop cloth over her carpet. Travis and Spence looked at her.

"What?" she said when she saw them looking. "I don't want y'all getting blood on my carpet."

When she was done, Travis and Spence tied Rex to a chair with his hands behind his back, and then they put duct tape over his mouth. Then Jackie walked up to Rex and slapped him in the face.

"You're gonna die, but not before you tell me where I can find Rob Berry."

Then Jackie sat down on the couch, made herself comfortable, and nodded at Travis. He put on his gloves and walked up to Rex.

"Time to bring the pain."

And with that, Travis went to work on him. He had been trained in interrogation techniques by Nick and Xavier and had learned his lesson well. After a while, Spence came and sat down next to Jackie.

"Your boy is really good at this."

"He damn sure is," Jackie said as Travis continued to bring the pain.

While Travis did his work, Spence's mind began to drift away from the task at hand. His mind was on Carolina Royce. After months of begging her to see him, Carolina had finally agreed to meet Spence earlier that night. She had feelings for Spence; there was no way that Carolina could deny that. "But you killed my man, Spence. How you expect me to feel?" she asked.

"Walt needed to die. He wasn't good to you or good for you. I want to give you the world, Carolina. Not have you waiting tables for me while I fuck everything with a pulse."

Carolina really couldn't say anything behind that, because it was the truth. She had been waiting tables for years at a club that her so-called man owned. Carolina had known, but never liked the fact that Big Walt's appetite for the ladies was legendary. And she had grown weary of the occasional ass kicking she took from him.

She exhaled and looked at Spence. "I know you were just following orders," Carolina began, but Spence cut her off.

"You don't understand. I didn't kill Walt because they told me to. I love you, Carolina. I killed him for you."

"What?" a surprised Carolina asked.

"I told you that I was done with him putting his hands on you."

"That's why you killed him?" Carolina asked, not sure of how she felt about that.

On one hand, she was still angry about the fact that, bastard or not, ass kicking or not, Walt was her man and she had loved him very much once.

That was before he started slapping me around because I asked him about one of his women.

And on the other hand, Spence had always been good to her. Over the years, he had treated Carolina the way she thought a man should treat her. In her life, Carolina had always wanted the bad boy, the drug dealer, the thug, and she usually got them. But she had also had her share of wannabe gangsters, fake niggas, and bottom feeders. What Carolina had never had was a man who loved her and only her. Now she looked at Spence and wondered if he would be any different.

Jackie sat quietly for over an hour and watched while Travis worked on Rex. Problem was, Rex wasn't talking. Jackie had other things she had planned for the evening and she was tired of waiting for Travis to make him talk.

"He's not going to talk," Jackie said and stood up.

Travis took a deep breath and hit Rex again. He had taken off his shirt and had broken a sweat beating Rex. "I don't know, Jackie." Travis hit him again. "I think he's just about ready to talk."

"Fine. Call me if you get anything out of him. But either way, kill him when you're done and get rid of the body."

"Yes, mommy," Spence said and got up. "We promise to play nice with our new toy and clean up after ourselves."

Jackie walked toward the door. "I ain't your mommy."

After Jackie left the office, Spence took over the beating. Spence hit Rex in the face, took a step back, and walked

183

over to where Travis was sitting. "You know why Jackie was in such a rush to get outta here?"

"No clue."

Spence turned back to Rex. "You know where she's going?" But Rex was too out of it to answer.

"Maybe she was getting frustrated with Rex," Travis said and laughed. "Here I was doing some of my best work, and he ain't talking."

For the next hour, Travis and Spence took turns beating Rex without him breathing a single word. Now it was Travis who had gotten frustrated with Rex.

"You might as well tell me where Rob Berry is, 'cause one way or the other, you're gonna die here in this office," Travis said.

Rex spit in Travis's face. "Fuck you!"

Travis wiped the spit from his face and took out his gun. He raised his pistol and placed it gently between Rex's eyes. "No, fuck you." Travis pulled the trigger.

When Jackie left Spence and Travis in the office to finish off Rex, she went in the club, grabbed one of her men and told him that he was driving. "Where are we going?" he asked when he got in the car.

"Five seventeen Lexington Avenue."

Her destination for the night was a bar called Lexington Brass. With its floor-to-ceiling windows, Lexington Brass was designed to be spacious, but edgy. "Park somewhere close and keep your eyes open. I'll call when I'm done," Jackie said and went inside.

She looked around the bar until she spotted them. As Jackie made her way to the table, she wondered if she really wanted to be bothered with them at all.

"Evening, captain," Angel stood up and said when Jackie approached the table.

But each time she saw Angel and Avonte she got wet. Angel was wearing a Rachel Zoe leather-sequin, sheath dress. Angel hugged Jackie and then Avonte stood up. Her eyes opened wide and her mouth watered at the sight of Avonte in her Elizabeth and James Levinson dress with very revealing geometric blocks of sheer mesh.

"We were starting to think that you weren't going to come," Avonte said.

"Had some business to take care of," Jackie said and joined them at the table.

"Nasty business?" Avonte asked.

"Bloody business."

Avonte leaned closer and ran her hand down Jackie's leg. "That mean you saved the nasty business for us?"

"Behave yourself, Avonte. Let the captain relax and have a drink with us." Angel ran her tongue over her lips and looked at Jackie. "I'm having The Brass Martini with Absolut Elyx, Dolin dry vermouth, and a twist of lemon."

Jackie turned to Avonte. "What are you having?"

"A Citrus Kiss."

"What's that?" Jackie asked.

"It's Herradura Silver, yellow Chartreuse, grapefruit, and lemon," Avonte said and kissed Jackie on the cheek.

Jackie was a cognac drinker so neither of those drinks appealed to her. She glanced at the drink menu and saw a drink made with Hennessey, Cointreau and lemon.

"I'll have The Brass Sidecar," Jackie said, and Angel sent Avonte to get the drinks.

"You still want the steak tartare and parmesan truffle fries?"

"I would." Angel didn't take her eyes off of Jackie. "Thank you, Avonte."

After a couple of rounds of drinks, Jackie was ready to move the evening forward. She looked at Angel. "Let's get outta here."

"I think that's an excellent idea, captain."

"Where you wanna go?" Jackie asked.

"The Marriot down the street."

"Convenient."

"We have a suite there," Avonte said and Jackie stood up.

Angel and Avonte exchanged looks and without saying a word, they stood up, got their things, and headed for the exit. They had both been looking forward to getting with

Jackie since they'd met her, but Jackie was about business. That meant that pleasure only came when the job got done.

It took less than fifteen minutes to get to the Marriot and into Angel and Avonte's suite. As soon as Jackie walked in the room, she slid her Stella McCartney stand-collar wool jacket off of her shoulders and let it drop to the carpet. That left only her two holstered 9's, a black bustier, and textured wool pants.

"Are you ready, captain?" Angel whispered in her ear and began nibbling at her earlobe, rolling the diamond stud in Jackie's ear around on her tongue, and then sucking on the lobe. Jackie ran her hand across Angel's leg, and then she grabbed Angel's face and kissed her.

Angel stepped out of her pants and immediately went right back at Jackie. As quickly as she could, Avonte took off her dress.

"Damn, you are fine as hell," Jackie said and began sucking her nipple.

"I tried to tell you how fine she was," Angel said and attacked her other nipple.

Angel moved in to remove Jackie's pants; she stepped out of them leaving her black lace thong, black stilettos, and her guns. "You look sexy, just like that, baby," Angel said.

Avonte removed the bustier and had both off Jackie's titties pushed together and was sucking hard on her nipples. Jackie liked it and held Avonte's head in place with one hand and squeezed the other. Jackie moaned out loud, and that encouraged Avonte to continue. She took one of Jackie's nipples into her mouth and Angel quickly went for the other.

Jackie looked at Avonte while she sucked her nipple. "Come here. I wanna taste you."

Jackie finally took off her guns and soon both women joined her on the bed.

"Lay back, baby," Avonte said and lowered herself to Jackie's face.

She held onto the headboard for support, playfully lowering herself over Jackie's waiting mouth. Eventually, Jackie was tired of the games and pulled Avonte's hips down, holding her in place, and started to suck on her lips and clit. She was rough, but it was turning Avonte on.

Avonte rode her face, crying out with pleasure from it. Jackie's moans eventually turned into loud screams as Angel had pushed her legs apart, moved her thong aside, moistened two fingers with her lips, and inserted them in Jackie. Then she sucked on her clit and zoned in on her G-spot.

"You like that, captain?" she asked.

Jackie, who liked to be in control, held onto Angel's long hair; gripping it and guiding her in the way that she wanted to be pleasured. She felt her body begin to tremble as Angel sucked her clit and licked it with the tip of her tongue.

Angel looked up at Avonte. She had her legs spread wide, and Jackie was making her quiver in ecstasy with her fingers and her tongue. Avonte began to feel her body convulse, so she got down from there.

Jackie pushed Angel's head out from between her legs and pulled Angel up to her face. Avonte literally dove in between Jackie's legs and licked her with the flat of her tongue. When she slid her tongue inside of Jackie, her body began to quiver.

"Oooh, shit!"

That went on for a while until Jackie ordered Avonte to lie down on the bed. When Avonte laid down, Jackie buried her face between her thighs and didn't see Angel get out of bed and return strapped up. Avonte watched as Angel spread Jackie's cheeks and slammed it into her.

"Fuck!"

Angel smacked her ass as hard as she could, and Jackie lifted her head from between Avonte's thighs long enough to say, "That's right, bitch. Fuck that pussy."

Angel fucked Jackie hard; her hips rocking back and forth. Avonte lay there in complete ecstasy while Jackie worked magic with her tongue. Then Angel pulled completely out of her and then slammed into her again. Avonte was getting so turned on watching Angel slamming her body into Jackie, that she began squeezing her nipples while Jackie sucked her dry.

When it was over, Jackie got out of bed and got in the shower. When she came out, Angel and Avonte had fallen asleep in each other's arms. Jackie got dressed and looked at her watch.

"Still got time to roll by Flip's."

Then Jackie armed herself and left the room.

43

It had been three weeks since Black asked Jada to provide the ladies to work at Flip's spot. Two weeks since she returned to the gambling house with Zacaria, Chloe, Marisa, and Requia. Before they left the Kimberly Hotel, Jada had instructed her ladies on what to do once they arrived at Flip's on that first night.

"When we get there, ladies, I want you all to sit down at a table and speak quietly amongst yourselves. With the exception of Victor, do not make eye contact with any man in the room for any reason." Jada turned to Zacaria. "Zacaria, I want you to keep your eyes on me at all times. Even if that means you do not participate in chatting with the other ladies, your job is to watch me."

"Yes, Jada," Zacaria said.

"When I raise my finger, you get the ladies up and come to me," Jada told her.

That night, Jada sat back, sipped her French 75, and observed how things worked at Flip's. Once she had seen enough, Jada stood up and her takeover began. Jada was raised in pool halls, so she understood the mix of men, money, liquor, and women. And what she didn't already know going in, she learned and learned well. "I have been fortunate enough to have two of the best teachers in the world. Sasha Deverox and Mike Black."

She had been to gambling houses before and knew how most of them operated, and Flip's was no different. Jada thought that the way she and Black ran Paraíso was better. She began working the room. Jada started at the bar, introducing herself to the men that weren't gambling. And then it was time to introduce the ladies.

When Jada raised her finger, Zacaria tapped on the table twice and all four ladies stood up at once. That move was enough to get the attention of every man in the house.

Victor leaned toward Flip. "Showtime."

The ladies got in line and then they walked single file to where Jada was standing. Zacaria stood next to Jada. "Gentlemen, may I introduce you to Zacaria Patton, Chloe Bailey, Marisa Alvarez, and Requia Blanchard." Each lady stepped up as her name was called and then stepped off to the left.

Knowing that just about every man was watching, Jada turned, looked straight at Sonny Edwards, and walked the ladies in the direction of his table. Once again, Jada introduced herself and the ladies to the men gambling at the tables. Then Jada smiled.

"With the introductions made, gentlemen, I'll get out of your way. However, if you need anything, a drink or just somebody to chat with, please feel free to call on one of these lovely ladies. They will be more than happy to satisfy your every desire."

When Jada walked back to her table, the ladies spread out around the room, but Zacaria remained. She walked up to Sonny and offered to get him a drink. When Sonny refused, as Jada knew he would, Zacaria leaned close to Sonny.

"Ms. West would like to speak with you whenever you're free," Zacaria said discreetly and walked away.

It was hours later and not before his game broke up for the night, when Sonny got up and walked to Jada's table.

"I understand that you want to speak to me," Sonny said.

"Yes, I do. Won't you please sit down," Jada said. "I wanted to take a minute and get acquainted."

"I am well aware of who you are, Ms. West."

"Are you really?"

"Yes, I am."

"Then you have me at a disadvantage."

"Mr. Black speaks very highly of you, Ms. West."

"Does he now?" Jada smiled. "You know Mr. Black well, do you?"

"I've known Mr. Black a long time. He told me once that you were the most dangerous woman that he had ever met. And now that I've gotten to meet you, I understand why he said that." Sonny stood up. "Good night, Ms. West. I'm sure that as time goes by that you and I will become well acquainted."

"I am quite sure we will. Good night."

Since that first night, Jada had been there every night; and in that time, revenue was up fifty percent. At that point, Jada had literally taken over Flip's game and had everyone eating out of her hand, just as Victor knew she would.

Not that Jada was running the place, nor was she even remotely interested in trying; Flip still ran the house. He just made sure to run everything by Jada first. It took a few nights, but Sonny finally told Jada his name, and a few more nights before she had him charmed, too. With the exception of Simone, who still had other responsibilities to attend to, Jada had her entire team of ladies working at Flip's.

"Unless you have a client, your attendance at Flip's each evening is mandatory," Jada told them.

I CAME TO BRING THE PAIN

When Jackie came through the door, the first thing that hit her was how crowded the spot was that night. "This place is packed."

As Jackie walked around and spoke to the gamblers, she noticed that there were a lot of new faces in the house. There were also quite a few that had been there before, but they weren't regulars. During the entire time that she'd been in charge of running the game, Jackie had never seen the house packed like it was that night.

It was then that she saw the ladies. Jackie stopped in her tracks and counted eight ladies working the room. Then she saw Jada seated at a table, holding court with two of the players that always spent big money. Jackie turned quickly and headed for the office. When she got in there, Flip was in there with Victor.

"You wanna tell me what Jada West is doing here?"

"Don't you remember, Black told her to recruit the women to work here," Flip said.

"That was three weeks ago, Flip. What is she doing here tonight?"

Before Flip could answer, Sonny came in the office. "She's making you money, that's what she's doing here."

"What you talkin' about, Sonny?"

"You walked through the house; you saw how packed this place is."

"And?"

"And that's because of her and those ladies she came in here with. They've made all the difference in the world," Sonny said.

"She's a money maker, Jackie," Flip said.

"So y'all just let her come in here and takeover my spot?"

Sonny sat down. "Flip, Victor, why don't you two give us a minute."

Both Flip and Victor got up and left the office. Once they were gone, Jackie stood in front of Sonny.

"Let me straighten you, young lady. This is not your game. This game belongs to Mike Black. It was Mike Black's game when he allowed you to run it for him. It was Mike Black's game when Wanda took it away from you, and it was his game when he handed it back to you. The world you are permitted to exist in belongs to Mike Black. Am I making myself clear, Jackie?"

"Yes, Sonny, you're making yourself clear," Jackie said because she respected Sonny and she knew that he was right.

"That's good to know. Now be clear about this; if Mike Black wants that woman in here, then you need to shut the fuck up and accept it. Besides, all she's doing is making you money."

"She is?"

"Yes, Jackie, she is. You think that woman has walked outta here with a single dollar those ladies have made?"

"She hasn't?"

"That women is not only loyal to Mike Black, she's in love with him. He told her what he needed her to do, and you can look and see how good a job she did getting it done."

"Does Black know what she's doing here?"

"Other than him telling her what he needed that night, no."

"Victor didn't tell him?"

"Victor works for her. So by definition, he must be loyal to her."

"So what you're sayin' is that if I want Black to know, then I need to tell him."

"Right."

Jackie leaned back in her chair. "Two things: I'm gonna tell Rain what's up and let her worry about it."

"Now you're thinking clearly. What's the second?"

"Shy already said that she was going to kill her, and sooner or later, she is gonna come through that door; and when she does, I hope you still know how to duck when she starts blasting."

44

In a very short time, Detective Mitchell was able to compile a lot of information about her suspect and then she shared it with Carmen.

"Tyhedra Crawford. Born October 15, 1978 in St. Louis, Missouri. She moved to Kansas City in 1999. The first of two cases were reported in 2001. In 2003, she moved to Dallas, Texas. She lived there for three years and over that time span, eight murders were reported. Move ahead to 2006, she moved to Phoenix."

"How long and how many?" Carmen asked.

"She was there for less than a year and two cases were reported. Then she moved to Vegas for five years."

Carmen laughed a little. "I know she got buck wild in Sin City."

"Twenty cases. Then it was off to LA; she killed three there. Then Atlanta and then here."

"Oh, no, not the ATL."

"Like the police in LA, Atlanta police figured it out, contacted LAPD, and they began showing that original sketch on the news. That's when our suspect moved here."

"That's a lot of moving. How does she support herself?"

"Tyhedra Crawford is a very successful business consultant."

"If you got all that, I know you have her address."

"The Caledonia on West 17th Street."

"In Chelsea?" Carmen asked.

"In Chelsea," Mitchell replied.

That night, the two investigators parked outside The Caledonia and waited. When they saw the suspect leave the building, Mitchell got out of the car and Carmen followed her. The detective went in the building, showed her badge to the doorman, and lied about where she was going. She went to her suspect's apartment, picked the lock, and went in. Mitchell searched the apartment. When she didn't find anything, she left the apartment and called Carmen.

"Where are you?"

"I'm at DBar on West 19th Street."

"What is she doing?"

"Sitting alone at the bar."

"Anybody approach her?"

"Two men sat down next to her, but she sent them away quick."

"I'm on my way. Call me if she leaves before I get there," Mitchell said.

"Will do," Carmen said and ended the call.

When Mitchell arrived at DBar, she joined Carmen at a table in the back. They sat there watching for the rest of the evening before Tyhedra paid her bar tab and went home.

It was more of the same the next night. Tyhedra went to Flight 151 on Eighth Avenue. Carmen and Mitchell sat and watched her drink alone and dismiss man after man all night long. The third night of their surveillance it was back to Pierre Loti, where they'd gotten the original information from the doorman. Fortunately, he wasn't working that night.

On night four her destination was The Tippler on West 15th Street. As they'd done for the past three nights, Mitchell and Carmen sat and watched from a distance. But this night was different. They watched Tyhedra eyeing a man for a while before he sent her a drink. When she motioned for him to join her, the investigators got excited.

"Tonight might be the night."

Predator and prey talked at the bar for a while, and then Tyhedra got up and moved to a table in the back of the bar. Before long, the prey arrived at the table with drinks and they talked some more. After that, Tyhedra stood up and walked in the direction of the ladies room. When the prey left the bar, Mitchell and Carmen thought that this was going to be another wasted night.

"Wait a minute, Diane," Carmen said. "She didn't go in the bathroom."

They sat there and watched as she sat down at a table and watched him leave the bar. Then she went to the bar and then left.

"That's why nobody's seen her leave with anybody. She waits to be sure that nobody in the place would be able to connect her to leaving with her victim before she leaves the bar. "Come on," Mitchell said, and they grabbed their things and followed her out of the bar.

When they got outside, the detective and Carmen watched as predator and prey talked and then left in separate cars. Mitchell and Carmen followed Tyhedra Crawford and her prey for the evening to the Bowery Grand Hotel. They continued to look on as he went in the hotel while she remained in her car. Then he went to the room by himself, and she went up to the door shortly thereafter.

"She's good," Carmen said.

"And careful," Mitchell added.

While Carmen stood back, Mitchell readied her weapon and then she started banging on the door.

"Police!—Open this door right now!"

After a while, the door opened and the prey stood there looking confused. "Is there a problem officer?"

"Let me see some ID," Mitchell demanded. He took out his driver's license. "Maurice Lennon." Mitchell looked at the ring on his finger. "I suggest you go on home to your wife. You can thank me later. Now, get your shit and get out of here."

Once he'd left the room, Mitchell came in with Carmen. She closed the door behind them while Mitchell approached the suspect.

"I'm Detective Mitchell. Can I see some ID, please?"

"I don't have any on me."

"That's okay. I already know everything I need to know about you, Tyhedra."

"Do you mind telling me what this is about?" she asked with a faked look of outrage on her face.

"Not at all. Your name is Tyhedra Crawford. You're a business consultant and you live at The Caledonia. And you're a serial killer that is wanted for murder in six states." The outraged look on Tyhedra's face washed away. "Now, let's start over. I'm Detective Mitchell. Can I see some ID, please?"

"It's in my purse." Tyhedra stood up.

"Stop."

Mitchell went and got the purse. The detective held it open and checked it for weapons before allowing Tyhedra to get her license and hand it to the detective.

"Thank you." Mitchell glanced at it and put the license in her pocket. "I'm gonna hold on to this."

From there, Mitchell reviewed for Tyhedra exactly what she'd been doing since she arrived in New York from Atlanta.

When her prey for the evening wasn't looking, she had placed her gun under the pillow. If she could get to it, Tyhedra thought she might have a chance to get out of this. Tyhedra sat down on the bed.

"So what happens now?" she asked.

"Normally, I would arrest you for murder," Mitchell said and took her eyes off of Tyhedra for just a second.

When she did, Tyhedra reached and grabbed her gun from under the pillow. The move caught Mitchell completely off guard. Before she could react, Tyhedra was off the bed and had a gun at the detectives head.

"Now, nice and easy and with your left hand, take your gun out of the holster and toss it on the bed."

Mitchell very slowly and carefully complied with Tyhedra's orders.

"Good. Move away from the door, Carmen Taylor. And please don't do anything stupid. I would really hate to kill you," Tyhedra said.

"Do what she says, Carmen," Mitchell said.

Carmen held her hands out in front of her and began to move away from the door. With her gun pressed against Mitchell's temple, Tyhedra backed her way to the door. When she reached back to open the door, Tyhedra looked back quickly for the doorknob.

That gave Carmen enough time to dive on the bed, grab Mitchell's gun, and fire.

Carmen's shot hit Tyhedra in the head.

Detective Mitchell stepped away as Tyhedra's body slumped to the floor. She looked at Carmen. "You okay?" she asked.

"I'm okay. Thank you, Carmen." Mitchell bent down and took the gun from Tyhedra. Then she called it in. "I'm glad that you're a good shot."

Carmen laughed a little. "That criminal that you don't want me hanging around is the one that taught me how to save your life."

45

It was Bobby's son RJ's sixteenth birthday and his parents were giving him a party. In addition to some of the children's friends, mostly from their old neighborhood, Bobby had invited Black, Shy, and their children, who'd arrived in the city with M that morning. Perry, Glenda, their son Walter, their daughter Malia, and her finance, Houston Griffin, were also in attendance. Naturally, Rain was there, as was Howard and his wife, Evelyn, and Sherman, and his wife, Ester. And since they were going to be there anyway, Pam invited Smoke and Napoleon. Even Jamaica had made it to town for the party.

Nick parked his Estoril blue crystal Audi R8 down the street from Bobby's house. Nick got out and walked around to the other side of the car, opened the door for April and extended his hand to her. She accepted his hand.

"Thank you, Nick."

Then he held the door open while Marvin got out of the backseat. Nick rang the doorbell and it wasn't too long before Pam opened the door.

"Hello, Pam," Nick said and hugged her. "I want you to meet Marvin Dancer and his mother, April."

"It's nice to meet you both. Come on in," Pam said and stepped aside so they could enter the house.

Marvin walked in the house and looked around the room. That's when he recognized RJ. He didn't know what his name was, but he knew that they went to the same school. Then he saw somebody else that he recognized. He didn't know her name either, but he had seen her around.

"Hey, Black," Rain said. "You hear what Sherman said?"

When Marvin heard her say Black, he looked to see who she was talking to. He saw Black standing with his arm around Shy and standing next to Bobby.

That's Mike Black, he whispered to himself, and then he looked at the man standing next to Black. *That's Bobby Ray. Wait a second, if that's Mike Black and Bobby Ray. . . .* Marvin looked at the man standing next to him. It was then that he realized who his father was. He had heard the stories about Nick and Freeze for years.

Marvin stood frozen as he watched Nick and his mother walk up to Black. Nick shook hands with Black and then Bobby. His mouth opened wide as Black stepped up and hugged April.

"Hi, Mike."

"Good to see you again, April."

April turned to Bobby. "Hi, Bobby. Thank you so much for inviting me," April said and looked around for Marvin. When she saw him standing there, April went and got him.

"Come here, Marvin. There are some people we want you to meet," she said and grabbed him by the hand.

As Rain looked on with fire in her eyes, April literally dragged Marvin to where Black, Bobby, and Nick were standing. She had heard that Nick was back from Yemen and knew that he would definitely be at RJ's party. Rain wanted to look her best, so she bought an outfit just for the occasion.

Nick saw her as soon as he walked in the room. He thought that she looked good in the Phillip Lim pleat-front top with satin and striped silk, straight-leg pants.

"This is my son, Marvin."

Bobby looked at Marvin, laughed and walked away; Black just stared at him. Both men wanted to intimidate the young man to see what he was made of, but they would take care of that later in the day.

"Hello, Marvin, I'm Mrs. Black. It's nice to meet you," she said and turned to April. They hugged one another. "Nice to see you again, April."

"Good to see you again, too, Mrs. Black."

"Please call me Shy," she said, and Black continued to look at Marvin without speaking.

"Shy it is. I love your outfit," April said of Shy's Yigal Azrouel leather and suede jacket and stretch leather pants.

"Thank you, April. You look very nice, too." April wore a St. John Annabel bootleg pants and elbow-sleeve top.

Shy whispered something in his ear, and it was only then that Black held out his hand to a still wide-eyed Marvin. April nudged her son and he shook Black's hand. After that, Nick led them away and introduced April and Marvin to some of the other guests.

Rain walked up to Black. He saw the look on her face. "Did I really hear what I thought I did?"

Black nodded his head.

"Then that is really Nick's son?"

"Yes." Black put his drink down and looked at Rain. "Don't kill them."

"I won't."

"You outta here?"

"Yeah," Rain said and walked away.

Shy shook her head. "None of y'all thought to tell her they were coming?"

"How was I supposed to know that he was gonna bring them?" Shy rolled her eyes and walked away.

Rain walked up to Bobby and Pam. She told them that she had to go and thanked them for inviting her. Then she stepped to RJ and handed him a couple of hundred dollar bills.

"Happy birthday, RJ."

Nick watched as Rain hugged RJ, kissed him on the cheek, and quickly left the house.

46

When Shy left Black alone, she went in the family room where most of the women were and sat down. Black signaled for Smoke to come to him. "Follow her. Let her have her space, but make sure nothing happens to her," Black ordered, and Smoke went after Rain.

Then Black saw RJ and signaled for him to come and talk to him. "Yes, Uncle Mike," RJ said.

"You enjoying your party?"

"I sure am."

Black pointed at Marvin. "You know him?"

"I don't know him personally, but he goes to my new school. They call him Money Marv," RJ said.

"Why do they call him that?"

And for the first time in his life, RJ lied to his uncle. "I haven't been at that school long enough to know why."

"I want you to find out for me."

"I will, Uncle Mike."

Just then, Easy ran into the family room and jumped in Shy's lap.

"You want me to get the little Prince, Uncle Mike?"

"In a minute, but I wanna tell you something first." Black looked at his son in Shy's lap and then back at RJ. "You know you were right when you said that one day you and Easy are gonna rule the world, just like me and your pops do now."

"I know, Uncle Mike. And I promise you that you ain't ever gotta worry about anything happening to Easy while I'm around."

"I have no doubt that you will look out for him. But you see, RJ, it's more than that. It's not just you and Easy that are going to take over all this. It's Michelle, and Barbara and Belinda, and Bonita, too. Do you understand what a huge responsibility that is?"

"Yes, sir."

"You're a man now, RJ. Easy is just a little boy, so the responsibility falls to you. I expect you to look out for and protect your sisters and my children."

"I won't let you down, Uncle Mike."

"I know. I have confidence in you, RJ."

"You can count on me. I'll die before I let anything happen to any member of my family."

Black laughed a little. "You sound like your pop now."

"My pop's a great man."

"The best man I know. You'll be lucky if you can find a friend like I found in your father," Black said. "I wanted to get you something special for your birthday, but your Aunt Shy, your mother and your pop, wouldn't let me. So I'll give you this instead." Black handed him an envelope with ten one hundred dollar bills in it.

"Thanks, Uncle Mike."

"And I'll show you this." Black showed RJ a Smith & Wesson Model M&P22 pistol. "It's yours. I'll just hold on to it for a couple of years."

"Thanks, Uncle Mike. I swear, you will always be able to count on me."

Black hugged RJ. "Happy birthday."

As RJ walked, the young man was feeling ten feet tall. His uncle had told him exactly what he wanted to hear on his sixteenth birthday. As far as RJ was concerned, the day couldn't get any better.

"Can I have everybody's attention, please?" Pam grabbed Bobby by the hand and moved to the middle of the floor. "I wanted to thank everybody for coming to celebrate our son's sixteenth birthday."

"Come here, RJ," Bobby said, and his son came and stood with his parents. Then Barbara, Belinda, and Bonita came and joined them. Barbara was carrying a big gift wrapped box; she handed it to Pam. "Happy birthday, RJ."

Everybody clapped as RJ ripped the paper off of the box and opened it. Everybody laughed when he pulled out another gift wrapped box.

"Wow, just what I wanted, a box," RJ joked. Once again the birthday boy tore the wrapping paper off and opened the box, only to reveal a smaller, gift wrapped box.

"Don't look at me; you know I didn't do all that wrapping," Bobby said, and RJ continued opening boxes until he got down to one small box.

RJ held up the box. "I hope this is what I think it is," he said, then held the box to his ear and shook it. "It is!" RJ shouted and ripped open the box. "It's the keys to a car!" RJ shouted and held up the keys. "What is it?"

"I think you should put a coat on, go outside and see," Pam said.

RJ grabbed his coat and rushed outside; held up the keys and pressed the alarm. Then RJ, with a small crowd led by Bobby and Pam following behind him, kept pressing the alarm until the lights flashed on a Dodge Charger. He turned around and hugged his parents. "Thank you, Mommy. Thank you, Pop."

"You're welcome, RJ," Pam said and kissed him on the cheek. "Just drive safely."

"I will, Mommy. Come on and ride with me. You'll see; I'm a safe driver." RJ looked at Bobby. "You too, Pop."

"You go ahead with your mother. Me and you got plenty of time to ride together."

"I wanna go," Barbara said.

"Me too," both Bonita and Belinda said. RJ held open the door for his mother and sisters before he got in and drove off.

Later that night, Nick whispered something to April. She nodded her head and walked away. Then Nick followed Bobby down the steps to the basement.

"RJ," Black said and motioned for him.

"Yes, Uncle Mike."

"Go get Easy and come downstairs."

"Yes, sir." RJ walked over to where Shy was sitting with Easy in her lap. "Easy."

Easy stopped and looked up at his cousin.

"Come with me," RJ said.

Shy laughed as Easy climbed down from her lap and followed RJ.

April walked over to where Marvin was sitting and asked him to come with her. They went down the stairs into the basement. When they got to the bottom of the steps, Nick was standing there. "I'll take it from here."

April turned and went back upstairs. Marvin looked around the room and saw that Black and Bobby were seated in front of him. RJ was sitting in between Black and Bobby and Easy was sitting still and quiet on the floor at his father's foot. Perry and his son, Walter, were sitting next to Bobby, and Jamaica stood in the back of the room.

"RJ," Black said and Bobby looked at him.

RJ smiled and then he got up slowly and walked toward Marvin. "I know I've seen you around school, but we've never been introduced. My name is Robert Ray Jr. and I want to thank you for coming and celebrating my birthday with me." He looked back at Bobby and pointed. "That man there is my father, Bobby Ray, and the man sitting next to him is my uncle, Mike Black. You know who they are, don't you?"

Marvin nodded his head.

"Answer the man," Nick said.

"Yes, I know who they are," Marvin said louder.

"Then you know who I am," Nick said and laughed. "Or at least who I used to be."

"Yes, sir, I do."

"My uncle asked me if I knew you," RJ began. "I told him no, but they call you Money Marv."

"Yeah." Marvin laughed a little, but nobody else laughed with him.

RJ stepped closer to him. "But I know why they call you that," he said softly.

"Like it or not, like us or not, you're a part of this family now. Every man in this room will die for you." Black stood up and walked toward Marvin. "So, tell me, *Money Marv*, why should we welcome you into this family?"

When Rain left Bobby's house, she was upset that Nick not only had a son, but he brought him and his mother to the party. She stopped at a liquor store and bought a pint of Patrón, rolled a couple of blunts, and drove around until she got to Babalu; a Latin restaurant and lounge on East Tremont Avenue. Not only was she feeling Latin and musical, Rain was fucked up and she was hungry, so she went in.

"Patrón," she told the waitress as soon as she walked up. She handed Rain a menu and walked away. When she returned with the drink, Rain ordered Moqueca Brazilena, a dish made with snapper, jumbo shrimp, scallops and calamari, fresh coconut, yuca and moqueca sauce.

While she ate and drank, Rain realized that Nick had every right to bring his son with him. She had to remember that despite everything that had happened in the past and with what was going on then, that this was Nick's family. She was the outsider trying to carve out a place for herself. Rain knew that she had earned everybody's respect, and as a result of that respect, she had earned her place in the family.

Rain finished her drink and was about to signal for the waitress to order another, when she saw Gee Cameron come in with three of his men.

"Shit."

Rain dropped her head and hoped that they didn't see her. Since she was going to a party at Bobby's house and everybody there was armed, Rain only had one gun and one extra clip on her.

"Can I get you another drink, honey?" the waitress asked.

"Patrón. And bring the check."

Rain dismissed the waitress and kept her eyes on Cameron and his men as they went to the bar and sat down. When the waitress returned with her drink and the check, Rain paid her with a hundred dollar bill. "Keep the change."

"Thanks, honey," the waitress said excitedly.

"Where's the ladies room?"

"Right over there." The waitress pointed.

Rain looked in that direction and saw the sign. She would have to pass the bar to get there, but she could make it.

"Is there an exit back there?"

"An alarm will go off, but yeah, there's a back door." The waitress began to clear the table. "Man trouble, honey?"

"You just don't know," Rain replied and kept her eyes on Cameron.

The bartender had just placed the drink in front of Cameron when he spotted Rain out of the corner of his eye. He smiled at her and raised his glass. Rain eased her gun out of her purse and made sure that she had one in the chamber.

Then she watched as Cameron said something to his men. While they finished their drinks, Rain gave some thought to the fact that she wouldn't be in this spot if she hadn't let Nick's showing up with his son get to her.

"Shit."

If she really wanted to be honest with herself, Rain would have to admit that it wasn't Nick coming there with

Marvin that was bothering her. It was the fact that he came with April that set her off.

When Cameron's men got up, Rain readied herself because she knew it was her time to die and she was determined to go out blasting, taking some of them mutha fuckas with her.

Then one by one, they each shook hands with Cameron and headed out of Babalu. Once they were gone, Cameron looked at Rain and then he stood up and walked over to her table.

"Mind if I sit down?"

"Not at all," Rain said, and Cameron sat down.

"So what's up?"

"You tell me, Gee; what's up?"

"I ain't here to kill you."

"I kinda figured that when your boyz didn't come over here and escort me out at gunpoint. Then you sent them away and came over here and sat down. I figure they're outside waitin' for me to come out so they can kill me."

"Nothing like that. I just wanted to talk."

"Okay, go ahead and talk."

"I wanna know why you made me think we was cool, when all the while you was playin' me?"

Rain was taken by surprise by what he said, but she went with it anyway. "We *are* cool, Gee. But this is business."

"I know that. But damn, Rain, I thought we had moved past that shit."

"I didn't kill you, did I?"

"No, you didn't, and I know damn well that you could have."

"Look, Gee, it's like this. Them King's had that mutha fucka, Monk kill Black's baby mama. What you think Black was gonna do? Shit, he wanted all of y'all mutha fuckas dead. But I went to Black and told him that we was cool and that I wanted you with me. But now, you with that nigga Rob Berry, so now all bets is off. I gotta do what I gotta do. I gotta kill both of you now."

"What happens then?"

"All the shit y'all got is mine."

Cameron finished his drink and signaled for the waitress. "Bring me a Bombay Sapphire and tonic. And bring the lady a shot of Patrón."

"You all right, honey?"

"I'm cool." Rain nodded and the waitress went to get the drinks.

"Since we still cool, if I wasn't with Berry, if I was to come around to your way of thinking, where do you see me?"

Rain leaned forward. She still had her gun in her hand under the table and was ready to kill Cameron anytime she didn't like where the conversation was going. "Where you wanna be?"

"Right next to you."

Rain sat back and laughed. "Nobody stands next to me. Nobody." Then she smiled. "Because we cool, I was thinking under me might be a good place for you. I like being on top," Rain teased.

"Yeah," Cameron nodded his head. "Under you is exactly where I want to be."

The waitress returned with their drinks.

"How bad you wanna be there?" Rain asked as soon as the waitress was gone. "I mean, my deal ain't changed. I'm offering you control of the whole show."

"And I kick up to you," Cameron said.

Rain nodded.

"Here's what I got to offer. I put you in position to kill Rob Berry, you give me a couple of hundred grand and control of everything that Rob got. And you."

Rain laughed. "You had a deal until you decided to make me part of it."

"Then we got a deal. We'll discuss the matter of you and me another time."

"Deal." Rain finished her drink, put away her gun so Cameron couldn't see it, and then she stood up. "Let's go." Her plan was to tell Cameron that her gun was in the car and then kill him once they got there.

"Now?"

"Yeah, now nigga. If you can put me in front of Rob Berry, we gonna do it now or the deal is off and we go back to trying to kill each other."

Cameron drained his glass and got up. "Let's go."

48

When Rain walked past him, Cameron paused to admire the way she looked in the Phillip Lim outfit that she had on. "You look so fuckin' hot in that," he said.

"Your ass is just sayin' that 'cause you want some of this pussy."

"Yes, I do."

Cameron tried to hug Rain, but she pushed him off of her.

"Let's go take care of this business and then we'll see just how bad you really want this pussy." Rain started walking toward the door. "'Cause I'll be honest with you, I don't think you really want any parts of this pussy. I guarantee you that you ain't ready for everything that comes with this pussy."

"That's where you're wrong. I want everything that comes with that pussy."

It was when Rain came outside of Babalu's that she saw Smoke's car parked across the street. Now that Smoke was there, Rain changed the plan. With Smoke backing her play, Rain decided that she would let Cameron walk her into Sweet Nectar and kill Rob Berry. Once Berry was dead, she would kill Cameron, too.

When Rain got to the car, she went into the trunk and got another 9mm and a Mac Ten. Even though it was cold outside, she took off her coat and began unbuttoning her pleat-front top. "Turn around."

"No," Cameron smiled and kept watching as Rain took off her blouse and put on her bullet-proof vest. "And all this time I thought you were invincible."

"I am invincible," Rain pounded the vest, "because I wear this fuckin' vest."

She put her coat back on; put the Mac Ten under it and a 9mm in each pocket. Then Rain put on her blonde wig and glasses. "Let's go."

When they arrived at Sweet Nectar, Cameron was able to walk Rain in without any problems. Smoke got out of his car, got his Uzi from the trunk, and followed her in. He took a seat at the bar and waited for the shooting to start.

After he got her a drink, as promised, Cameron walked Rain to the back of the club where Rob Berry was seated in a booth with two other men and four women. When Berry saw Cameron coming toward the table, he sent the ladies away.

"What's up, Gee?"

"I just wanted to introduce you to somebody," Cameron said.

"Who's that?" Berry asked.

"Rain Robinson."

Rain dropped her drink, pulled the Mac Ten from under her coat, and sprayed the booth with bullets. Rob Berry and the men in the booth were dead.

Cameron pulled his weapon and began firing as more of Berry's men began firing at him and Rain. She turned around and returned fire and began making her away toward the door. As they got closer, Smoke pulled out the Uzi and began clearing a path toward the door.

Once they were outside, Cameron ran for his car. He was a little surprised when Rain got in the car with Smoke. He followed Smoke's car until they were back at Rain's car at Babalu's. On the way there, Rain had decided just how she was going to kill Gee Cameron.

"Stay with me, but keep outta sight," Rain told Smoke and she got out.

Rain walked up to Cameron's car. "You'll have your money in the morning," she said and started to walk away.

"I thought we were gonna talk about you and me?" Cameron said as Rain walked.

"What's to talk about? Just follow me and we'll see if you really are ready for all this," Rain said and kept walking to her car.

Once they got to the room, Rain tossed her purse on the bed, and then she took off her coat and the vest. Rain slapped her titties and stepped up the Cameron. He tried to kiss her and began fumbling with his belt. Rain squeezed her breasts until Cameron's pants were undone and around his ankles.

Rain slid her hand across his dick. "I guess this will do." She pushed him down on the bed.

Rain stepped out of her satin and striped silk, straight-leg pants, and slid her panties to one side and began massaging her clit. She moaned from the pleasure she was giving herself. Then Rain leaned over the bed, reached for her purse, and pulled out a three-pack of condoms. She tossed them at Cameron.

"What are you waiting for?"

While Cameron excitedly put on a condom, Rain reached in the purse and positioned her gun where she could get to it. Then she spread her lips and played with her clit while Cameron got the condom on and began stroking his dick.

Rain got on top of Cameron and slid down on him. He grabbed her hips and pushed his dick inside her as hard as he could. With her eyes squeezed tightly shut, Rain rode him hard and thought about Nick. In her mind it was Nick that she was grinding her hips into.

Damn, this dick is so fuckin' good, she thought, even though it wasn't. She was thinking about Nick slamming himself in and out of her; furiously pounding her juicy pussy until her body started to tremble. Rain began to buck harder and harder, squeezing her breast with one hand and holding her ass with the other.

"Yeah," Cameron said as Rain sat straight up on him, and rode him as hard as she would if it actually were Nick that she was on top of.

Cameron grabbed Rain's hips and closed his eyes. With his eyes closed, he didn't see Rain lean to one side and take the gun out of her purse. She began to move faster as her head drifted back and her eyes opened wide.

Rain got off of Cameron and put the barrel of her gun to his head.

"Nigga, that wasn't shit."

Rain pulled the trigger.

49

The following night, Black and Shy took M, Michelle, and Easy to the airport for their flight back to Freeport. Once they were on their way safely out of the country, Shy asked Black what was on his agenda for the evening. "I'm going to roll by Impressions and meet Rain. I heard she got herself into a little trouble last night after she left Bobby's house. I wanna hear what she has to say."

"I knew she was hurt and on her way to getting herself into trouble."

"I did, too. That's why I sent Smoke to follow her."

"You mind if I ride with you?"

"Not at all."

"Good. I told Dale that I would meet her someplace."

"If you're hanging out with Ryder tonight, you make sure Napoleon doesn't leave your sight."

"Yes, baby."

A few hours later, while Shy waited at the bar with Napoleon for Ryder to get there, Black was in the office with Bobby and Rain.

"I got Gee Cameron to walk me up in Rob Berry's spot and I killed him, and then I killed Gee."

"I'm dying to hear how you did that," Bobby said.

Rain leaned back and held her breasts.

"These mutha fuckas work miracles on weak niggas."

All three laughed.

"We need to roll around to some of their spots and make sure everybody knows they're dead and it's a new day," Black said,

"I'll take Smoke and hit some spots," Bobby said.

"That works." Black got up and left the office. Bobby and Rain followed him out. When Bobby came into the club, he found Smoke and told him what they were going to do, and then they left Impressions.

Black went to the bar to talk to Shy just as Ryder walked up. "What's up, Dale?"

"I'm good, Sandy," Ryder said and gave Shy a little hug.

"Cassandra," Black said when he got to the bar.

"Hey, baby."

"I need to go somewhere with Rain." Black looked at Ryder. "How you doing, Ryder? I've been hearing good things about you."

"I try to do my work and do it good."

While Shy talked to Black, Ryder stood and watched as Rain waited for Black to get finished. Rain was wearing an Adam Lippes silk trench coat over an Alice + Olivia leather bell pants, and a Cass Peasant top with her vest under it. Then Black kissed Shy and then left with Rain. Ryder watched Black and Rain walk away and waited for Shy to come back to her.

"You ready to go?" Shy asked.

"Yeah, let's go."

Shy motioned for Napoleon to come on and walked off with Ryder.

"I gotta be honest with you, Sandy, that is one fine ass man you got."

Shy stopped and looked at her.

"Don't you look at me like that, Sandy," Ryder said. "I'm a real bitch. I ain't one of them *snaky bitches* that's always trying to sneak behind your back and fuck your man."

"I didn't say you were," Shy said and walked off.

"You a trip, Sandy. Me and you go too far back for you to think some shit like that about me. All I was gonna ask was, you don't mind him hanging around with little Miss tits and ass there?"

"No, Dale, I trust Michael, and Rain Robinson is the last woman I gotta worry about."

"I know you trust your man, but do you trust the rest of these half naked, money hungry skanks?"

Shy stopped and opened the black MaxMara camel hair, wrap coat that she had on. "What them bitches got that I don't?" She held open the coat to reveal the white Prabal Gurung tuxedo wrap jacket and wide-leg tuxedo pants that hugged her hips. "And in case you didn't notice, I'm rockin' some girls, too," Shy said and then she shook her breasts.

"Whatever, Sandy."

Shy and Ryder walked out of Impressions and waited for the valet to bring the S63 AMG around front. Napoleon held the car door open and the ladies got in the backseat. "Where to, Mrs. Black?"

"Where're we going, Dale?"

"48 Lounge. It's on Avenue of the Americas," Ryder said and Napoleon drove off.

After a few minutes of silence Ryder leaned closer to Shy. "I can tell by that silly look you get on your face every time he walks up that he's knockin' a hole in your back."

Shy smiled, mostly because it was true. The love they made was extraordinary. Still, she wondered where Ryder was going with this.

"So ain't no bitch out there that you worried about?"

Shy glanced over at Ryder. "There is this one bitch that's after Michael," she said and quietly told her the story of the two nights she spent with Jada West.

"And you ain't let them kill her ass?"

Shy shook her head.

"I know you at least gave the bitch a good beat down?"

Once again, Shy shook her head.

"I woulda had to beat her ass down. That shit was disrespectful."

"Tell me about it. The bitch had one more time to come out her mouth wrong before I put a bullet in her brain," Shy said.

"Still, the bitch needs a beat down; and if you won't do it, tell me where the bitch at and I'll do it. And when I'm done with her, you can look down at her and laugh."

"Peninsula Hotel," Shy said quietly.

"Let's go beat the bitch down," Ryder suggested.

Shy took a long hard look at Ryder and then she shook her head. She pointed at Napoleon.

"You remember the days when we used to ride in cabs for free?" Ryder asked.

Shy laughed. "I remember. Those were good days. We had a lot of fun then."

"You ready?"

"For what?"

Ryder gave Shy a look.

"No." Shy smiled, shook her head and thought about it.

"I guess there ain't but one ride-or-die chick in this car," Ryder said as Napoleon slowed down to stop at a red light.

Shy looked at Ryder and then grabbed the handle. "On three."

"One—two—three!"

The car doors burst open and Shy and Ryder jumped out and ran up the street as fast as they could. Napoleon got out of the car and went after them. Shy and Ryder ran around the corner and ran toward a line of cabs.

Napoleon rounded the corner. Shy and Ryder jumped in the first cab they got to through the same door. Ryder jammed a twenty in the money slot. "Pull off and drive when we get out," she said.

Napoleon saw them get in. Shy and Ryder got out of the cab through the other door and crouched down by the cab in front of them.

"The woman gon' get herself killed and me along with her," Napoleon said when he saw the cab drive off, and he ran back for the car.

Once they saw that he was gone, Shy and Ryder stood up and got into another cab.

"Where to?"

"Peninsula Hotel on Fifth Avenue," Shy said.

On the way there, Shy thought about what they were going to do when they got there. Shy smiled. "I wanna send the bitch a message. So we're gonna chill at the bar for a while; have some fun. I say a few choice words to her and then we go to 48 Lounge."

"That's cool. But I still think we need to beat the bitch down. But you're the boss."

"No, I'm the bosses' wife. There is a difference."

However, when Shy and Ryder arrived at The Salon de Ning, they found that Jada West was not there. "The snotty bitch usually has a table reserved here."

"I don't see any tables with reserved signs on them."

Shy was about to go to the bar and ask if she'd been in, but then she thought about the fact that her and Jada shot up the place that night. It was only logical that Jada would find someplace else to do business.

And then Shy thought about it. "We need to get outta here." Shy started walking quickly toward the exit.

Ryder followed behind her. "What's wrong?"

"Last time I was here, me and that bitch shot up the place."

"Okay, gangster."

On the way down in the elevator, Shy's phone rang. She looked at the display. "Oh shit."

"Who is it?"

"Michael." Shy said and pressed talk. "Hi, baby."

"Where are you?" Black asked.

"On our way to the 48 Lounge," Shy said innocently.

"Good. Napoleon is there waiting for you." Then Black ended the call.

When they got to the 48 Lounge, Shy and Ryder got out of the cab. As soon as they exited the cab, some men that were parked in a car across the street opened up on them. Quickly, the ladies took cover behind a car and took out there guns; the people that were standing in line scattered. Shy and Ryder were okay, but they were pinned down.

"I guess this is why you got a bodyguard," Ryder said and laughed a little.

"Shut up, Dale," Shy shouted. She looked at Ryder and then she laughed a little. "You ready?"

"Let's do it."

Shy and Ryder rose up from behind the car and opened fire on their attackers.

Inside the 48 Lounge, Napoleon heard the shooting outside and rushed out the door. Once he was outside, he looked toward where the shooting was coming from. As he expected, he saw Shy blasting away.

"The woman gon' get herself killed and me along with her."

Napoleon ran in the opposite direction toward the S63. He got in, started up, and headed for the action. Napoleon drove the car down Avenue of the Americas and skidded to a stop in front of the attackers. He jumped out and began laying down cover fire with two guns, in the hope that it would give them time to make it to the car.

As he expected, Napoleon drew the fire from the attackers. Still hiding behind a car, Shy noticed that their attackers weren't shooting at them. She looked around and saw that Napoleon was in the middle of the street and was shooting it out with their attackers.

"We gotta try to make it to the car."

"Okay, let's go!"

Napoleon kept firing while the ladies ran out from behind the car. They fired shots as they ran and jumped in the backseat of the car. Shy rolled down their window and fired to give Napoleon cover. He got behind the wheel, floored it, rounded the corner and sped away.

"I guess this is why the boss insist that you have a bodyguard, Mrs. Black."

"Shut up, Napoleon," Shy said and folded her arms across her chest.

51

Since Black didn't seem to have anything else for him to do, Nick went back to work. As always, the first person that he saw when he came in that morning was April. She was in the break room getting coffee.

"Good morning, April," he said and it startled her.

She spun around. "I told you about sneaking up on me like I'm some terrorist."

Nick looked at her without speaking. He had noticed that what April wore to work had changed since her husband, Marvin, had moved out. That day, April was looking very sexy in her Nanette Lepore supernova jacket, beaded silk top, and galaxy skirt that showed more thigh than he'd become accustomed to seeing on her. And he wasn't complaining. April's legs looked amazing in the opaque tights that led to a pair of Giuseppe Zanotti leather zip-front ankle boots.

"Nick?"

"Yeah."

"Good morning," April said, and that seemed to be enough to bring Nick out of the trance her outfit had him in.

"You look nice, April; very nice today."

"Thank you, Nick," she said and turned to finish making her coffee.

Nick continued to look and April could feel his eyes on her. In her mind, his eyes exploring every inch of her felt like hands on her body.

"So, what's on our agenda for today?" Nick finally asked, even though he knew. April picked up her coffee cup and told Nick in detail how their day was going to go, even though she knew he knew.

At the end of the day, things had gone exactly the way April said they would. They were sitting in April's office reviewing the day and making plans for the next.

"I'm getting ready to get outta here for the night."

Nick stood up and so did April.

"Me too," she said.

Nick took another look at April as she came around the desk and remembered that several times during the day, he was about to ask her to have dinner with him that night, but he was interrupted by one thing or another each time.

"Are you doing anything tonight, April?"

"Not really. I have some things that I was going to do around the house, that's all? Why, you need me to work on something?"

"No, no, April. Nothing like that. I was going to ask if you wanted to have dinner with me."

"Tonight?

"If you're too busy, I understand," Nick told her.

"No, no, tonight is fine," April said and immediately began thinking about what to wear on her first date with Nick. April smiled at him. "Our first date."

"How is this our first date? We've been out to dinner plenty of times."

"This is the first time you asked me to have dinner with you," April said, and Nick looked confused. "Don't you get it? Every other time we've gone out, you've just said 'let's go eat,' and we go. This time you asked me."

Whatever, Nick thought but didn't say. "I understand," he said even though he didn't.

Nick and April left the office and went down in the elevator. When they got to the lobby, April went one way as Nick went another. "Where are you going?" Nick asked.

"I'm going home to get ready."

"For what?"

"For dinner. Remember, you just asked me to dinner. So I'm going home to get ready and you're going to come and pick me up at my house." April turned to walk away, but then she turned back quickly. "What time should I expect you?"

"Seven o'clock."

April smiled. "See you at seven."

At exactly seven o'clock, Nick got out of his car and went to ring the doorbell. Nick's eyes opened wide when April opened the door wearing an M Missoni floral jacquard dress, and Kate Spade New York justice lace, slingback pumps. "Come in, Nick."

"You look beautiful."

"Thank you, Nick. You look very handsome, too," April said and stepped closer to straighten his tie.

"Is Marvin here? I wanted to say hello before we left."

"No, he's not. RJ came to pick him up," April said and got her coat. "They've been hanging out a lot since they met at the party."

"RJ's a good kid, so I guess that's all right."

"So, where are we going?"

"Anywhere you want."

"You know where I've always wanted to go?"

"Where?"

"Cuisine."

Nick let out a little laugh. "You've never been to Cuisine?"

"No never," April said shyly.

"Cuisine it is then," Nick said and helped April on with her coat. Then the two walked hand in hand to his car.

Meanwhile at Cuisine, Lexi, who had run Cuisine for Black for years, walked into the office. She stopped short when she saw that Black and Shy were seated on the couch.

"Oh–I didn't know you two were in here."

"We came in through the back door," Black said.

"We're sneaky like that," Shy added.

"Have a seat, Lexi. There's something I want to talk to you about."

Once Lexi was seated, Shy took a large envelope out of her purse. Black stood up and Shy handed him the envelope. He took out the papers, handed them to Lexi, and sat back down.

"What's this?" she asked.

"Just something I had Patrick draw up for you to sign," Black said as Lexi flipped pages. "Your signature on that document gives you one hundred percent ownership of this place."

"Okay. . ." Lexi said and continued to read. Then she stopped and looked at Black and Shy. "Wait, what did you say?"

"I said you own this place."

"What place?"

"This place."

"Cuisine?"

Black nodded his head and Shy smiled. "Congratulations, Lexi," Shy said.

"Oh my God! Thank you, Mike." Lexi got up and came around the desk. Black and Shy both stood up. And as tears rolled down her cheeks, Lexi hugged Black, and then she hugged Shy. "Thank you, Shy."

"You've earned it," Shy said; then she shed a tear as well. And Black felt good to see just how happy he had made Lexi.

At the same time that Black and Shy were leaving Cuisine through the back door, Nick and April arrived at the front door and were seated at a reserved table down in front.

"Your personal table?" April asked.

"Mike and Shy usually sit here," Nick explained.

Nick had just ordered the Caribbean lobster tail for himself and the steamed mussels tossed with a white wine sauce for April, when four of Brill's men came into Cuisine. Brill had gotten word that Black and Shy were there having dinner, and they had come there to kill them.

When the shooters barged into Cuisine, Lexi was just coming out of the office. As soon as she saw them she turned around and rushed back to her office. She took out her cell phone and called Black.

"Hey, Lexi," Shy said when she answered Black's phone.

"Four armed men just came in the club."

"What's wrong?" Black asked Shy.

"Four shooters in the club," Shy said and put the call on speaker.

"Are you all right?" Black asked as he turned the car around and headed back to Cuisine.

"I'm fine," she said, though she clearly wasn't. Having armed men roaming through what was now her club had her rattled, to say the least. "I'm in the office, Mike, but Nick is in the club."

"Don't worry about Nick. He can take care of himself. You go in the panic room and stay there. We'll be right there."

At the same time that Lexi was on the phone with Black and Shy, Nick saw the shooters come through the door; he turned to April. "Go to the ladies room, right now."

"Why, Nick?"

"Men with guns just came in. So get up and go to the ladies room now, please." April stood up. "And if you hear any shooting, get down on the floor."

"On the floor—in the ladies room—in this dress?" April asked jokingly as she hurried away from the table. She was almost there when the shooting started. Nick watched as April dove for the floor, and then she crawled the rest of the way.

Now that April was somewhat safe, Nick turned his attention to the bandits. One of Brill's men fired shots from his AK47 to get everybody's attention. Customers were screaming as they dove for the floor and covered their heads.

"We're looking for Mike Black!" the man that fired the shots yelled. His three partners spread out on the floor and began searching for him.

Outside of Cuisine, Shy got the PX4 Storm out of her purse and eased it in her pocket, and then she got out the PLR 22. Black brought the car to a screeching stop and they got out.

"Do you always carry a semi-automatic weapon with you wherever you go, gangster?" Black asked as they approached the club.

"Mike Black is my husband. Of course, I am armed at all times," Shy replied.

"You go around back," Black said and Shy frowned. "Make sure Lexi is okay and make sure nobody leaves." That was enough to make Shy smile as she went around back.

Black took a deep breath and opened the door slowly. When he got inside, he scanned the room and saw the bandits searching the club. Then he spotted Nick; he was crouched down and making his way to get a better angle on the shooters. Once they made eye contact, both men opened fire.

Black dropped to one knee, fired at a shooter, and caught him as he raised his weapon. Nick saw a man standing by the bar. He fired at Nick and he dove for the floor and returned fire, hitting the shooter twice in the chest. Nick walked up to him and kicked the gun away before shooting him in the head. Another man hit the floor and crawled to the front door. When he stood up and tried to make it out the door, Black took aim and hit him twice in the back.

Black and Nick began moving in on the remaining shooter. He grabbed a woman who was lying on the floor, and put a gun to her head. "Back off or I'll kill her," he said and started backing up toward the offices.

"Only way you're going to leave here alive is if you put the gun down and let the woman go," Black said, and he and Nick continued coming toward the gunman.

He looked over his shoulder and could see the back door. "I said back off or I swear I'll put a bullet in her brain."

I CAME TO BRING THE PAIN

Just then, Shy stepped out of the shadows and put her gun to his head. "No, you won't," she said and pulled the trigger when the man flinched.

Since Ellis had begun working for Brill, he'd been making money. More money than he had ever made in his life. He had felt bad living off of Scarlett these last few years, just not bad enough to get a real job and help out. The only money he had made was at the hands of Scarlett's father. Ellis knew it wouldn't be long before Scarlett got big time and divorced him. Until that time, he planned to suck Scarlett dry and make all the money he could with Brill.

That night, Scarlett had arranged to go to dinner at Black and Shy's house. When Ellis came through the door, Scarlett was getting ready. "Good, you're here. Hurry up and get dressed."

"Why? Where we going?"

"To Mike's house for dinner. He's cooking specially for us."

"I ain't going," Ellis told her, and thought about telling her that she couldn't go either.

"Why not, Ellis?" Scarlett asked as she continued to get ready to leave.

"I got shit to do."

"Like what?" Scarlett asked.

"That shit don't concern you."

"Whatever, Ellis."

After that, Scarlett finished getting ready and told Ellis of her plan to register Sherraine and Gordy at Onyx Academy of Higher Learning. "Mike and Shy send their children there."

"We don't need to do that right now while things are a little tight," Ellis said.

"The only reason things are a little tight right now is because *you* ran through *my* signing money."

Ellis's eyes narrowed and he stepped closer to Scarlett. "What you mean by that?"

"I'm talking about the new Lexus we didn't need, and the jewelry you're flashing around, the clothes you parade about in, and what about the pound of weed you been getting blasted off of every day."

For the next half an hour, Scarlett and Ellis went around and around about all the things they usually argued about. When the subject got back around to Mike Black and her new family was when Ellis started yelling. "You don't need to be gettin' involved with them people!"

"Them people? What are you saying, Ellis. He's my brother."

"How you know that?" Ellis yelled. "Huh, how you know that?"

"He's Daddy's son."

"Your daddy say he don't know nothing about havin' no fuckin' son named Mike Black."

"You talked to Daddy?"

"Yes. I do still work for him, you know. And he agrees with me, Scarlett. You don't need to be gettin' all up in their business."

"I don't know where all this is coming from, but Mike told me—" Scarlett began, but Ellis cut her off.

"And that's another fuckin' thing."

"What's that?"

"I'm gettin' tired of hearing about Mike this and Mike and Shy that. You spend too much time with those people, calling yourself working."

. "I am working. Mike wants me to do a show at Impressions, and I've been working with them on getting new material together. I told you that."

"That's what your lyin' ass mouth say, but you and I know what's really goin' on."

"Okay," Scarlett said. Once again, Ellis had hurt her with his words. She was a lot of things, but she wasn't a liar. "What's really going on?"

"That nigga ain't your brother. You fuckin' him, ain't you, Scarlett?"

"I know you didn't say that to me," Scarlet said as tears welled in the corners of her eyes. "I am not having sex with my own brother, Ellis. You really are crazy."

"Don't call me crazy!" Ellis yelled looking crazy.

"Calm down, Ellis. The children will hear you."

"I don't give a fuck!"

"There is nothing going on with me and Mike. Most days when I'm rehearsing at the club, Mike isn't even there. I'm just there working."

"I know what I know," Ellis said and their argument only escalated from there.

The two continued going back and forth until Scarlett had reached her boiling point. With tears rolling down her cheeks she looked at Ellis.

"I want a divorce."

"What'd you say?"

"I want a divorce," Scarlett said again.

That was when Ellis slapped the shit outta Scarlett and she grabbed her face.

"I'm outta here," Scarlett said and went to get her children.

"No, you ain't." Ellis grabbed Scarlett's arm.

"Yes I am," Scarlett said and broke out of his grip.

Scarlett turned around and started walking toward the children's room mumbling. "You're broke ass don't have any business telling anybody what they can't do."

Ellis ran up behind Scarlett and grabbed her by her hair.

"Ouch!"

Ellis slammed her face into the door and then he spun her around and started punching Scarlett in the face. She tried to run, but she couldn't move because he was still holding her hair and had her pinned against the door.

"You ain't going any damn where unless I tell you to!"

Ellis hit Scarlett again and then he let go of her hair. When he did, Scarlett slumped to the floor. Ellis kicked her a few times and then Scarlett got back up. Then she started throwing everything she could get her hands on at him, and then she ran. Ellis ran after her.

Scarlett made it to the kitchen with Ellis right on her heels. He chased her around the kitchen, and then Scarlett saw the pot of water on the stove. She picked it up and Ellis came at her. Scarlett hit him in the head with the pot. The impact of that blow caused Ellis to fall back and lose his balance. Then he slipped on the water that was now on the floor. Ellis hit the floor hard!

As quickly as she could, Scarlett got the children's coats and put them on. Then she grabbed her coat and got outta there. An hour later, a badly beaten and bloody Scarlett showed up at Black's house with the children.

"Oh my God!" Shy said when she answered the door. "Michael! Come quick!" she yelled and took Scarlett and the children in the house.

Black and Napoleon came running into the living room. "What's wrong, Cassandra," Black asked, and then he saw Scarlett.

Black stood there for a minute and then he went and sat next to Scarlett. Shy went to get something to clean off the blood. The children seem scared by everything that was happening around them, so Napoleon took them out of the room.

"Who did this to you?"

"Ellis."

Black's eyes narrowed. "Why?" he asked as Shy returned with a washcloth and some warm water. Once he got the children situated, Napoleon came back in the living room. He stood by the window and looked out.

As Shy gently wiped away the blood from her face, Scarlett told them what happened. "Do you think you killed him?" Shy asked.

"No. When I was leaving I saw him come out the door and get in his car."

"Why didn't you tell me that things weren't good with you and your husband?"

"I just met you both and you've been so good to me, I didn't want to burden you with my problems."

"I'm your brother, Scarlett."

"We're family," Shy said. "You can always come to us."

"Thank you."

"You should have told me," Black said.

"That's the thing, there was nothing to tell. We were doing good."

"What changed?" Shy asked.

"Things began to change after he found out that his friend, Walt, got killed. After that, he started hanging around with some guy named Lloyd."

That raised an eyebrow.

"Lloyd?" Shy asked.

"Brill," Black said.

"That's him."

Black stood up.

"Do you think he followed you here?" Shy asked.

"I don't think so. I drove around for a while before I came here."

"You were coming here for dinner. Do you think he'll come here looking for you?" Shy asked.

"If he does, I'll kill him." Black walked away and got his coat. "This shit ends tonight."

When Black got his guns, Shy and Napoleon got up and started to get ready.

"No," Black said. "You take her to Perry's and stay with her until you hear from me."

As Black left the house, slamming the door behind him, Shy and Napoleon looked at each other. "You know it's your fault the boss don't take us nowhere anymore."

"Shut up, Napoleon," Shy said.

"Okay, I shut up; but it is you with your bang, bang with your guns all the time."

Shy gave Napoleon the eye and then she looked at Scarlett. "We're gonna take you to get looked at by a doctor."

"Is he really going to kill Ellis?" Scarlett asked.

Once again, Shy and Napoleon looked at each other. "I'll get the children," Napoleon said and walked away.

Shy went and sat down next to Scarlett. "Yes, Scarlett. Michael is going to kill your husband and a lot of other people."

Black was mad as hell.

He walked out of his house thinking that there was a possibility that Brill might have been involved in what Ellis did to Scarlett. The idea that it may have been because of him, made Black want to hunt Ellis down and beat him to death. But since it was a short walk to Bobby's house, Black went there first.

Black took out his phone and called Rain. "What's up?" Rain asked.

"Meet me at Bobby's house, now."

"On my way." Rain ended the call.

Black walked up to Bobby's door, rang the bell, and the door swung open almost immediately.

"Oh," Bobby's oldest daughter Barbara said, sounding disappointed when she saw who it was. "Hi, Uncle Mike." She let him in and gave him a hug and a kiss on the cheek.

"Who were you expecting?" Black asked, and then he saw how short her dress was. "Where're you goin'?"

Barbara froze.

"She thought it was her boyfriend and she's dressed like that because she has a date," Pam said as she came in the room. "Hi, Mike," she said, and he kissed her on the cheek.

"Hey, Pam."

Black looked at Barbara. "You got a boyfriend?"

Barbara nodded her head. She was tall and slender like her father. Black looked at Pam; Barbara not only looked just like her mother, she was built like her too.

"How old are you again?"

"I'm almost fifteen, Uncle Mike," Barbara said and her voice went up a couple of octaves. "I'm not a little girl anymore."

"So I see." Black shook his head. Barbara was definitely not a little girl anymore. "Does your father know you got a boyfriend?"

"No, Uncle Mike, and please don't tell him," Barbara pleaded.

Black looked at Barbara and then to Pam. "Okay, but you and I need to talk about this boyfriend business."

"Thank you, Uncle Mike." Barbara kissed him and walked away.

"Dating?" Black said to Pam.

"They're going to the movies. I'm driving them there and picking them up when it's over," she said, because to her, Barbara going to the movies with a boy was no big deal.

"She's not a little girl anymore."

"Hasn't been for a while." Pam walked toward the steps. "You just never noticed." She smiled at Black. "Bobby's asleep. You want me to wake him up?"

"Yeah, Pam. Go ahead and wake him up."

Black went and sat down in the living room to wait for Bobby. It gave him a chance to think clearly. He was going to beat Ellis to death; there was no question or doubt in his mind about that. But if he wanted the war to end, and end that night, then he had to kill Brill. Something that—up until that point—hadn't proved easy to do.

It didn't take Black long to realize that the Walt Scarlett mentioned was Big Walt McDonald, and that's how Ellis got with Brill. That would be where he would look for Ellis first.

The doorbell rang and Black had to laugh as Barbara came running out of nowhere to answer the door.

"Hey, Cole," Barbara said.

"Hi, Barbara."

"Come in. I'll be ready in a minute." Barbara was about to close the door when she saw Rain rushing up the steps.

"Hold up, Barbara," Rain said.

"Hey, Aunt Rain." Barbara saw how Rain was looking at the young man. "Cole, this is my favorite aunt, Rain."

"Who this; your boyfriend?"

"Yes, Aunt Rain."

"Does your daddy know about this?"

"No, and we're not going to tell him and neither is Uncle Mike," Barbara said and led them into the living room. She was surprised when she saw Bobby sitting in there with Black.

"Tell me what, Barbara?" Bobby asked and looked Cole up and down.

"Daddy, Uncle Mike, this is my friend Cole," Barbara said nervously.

"They're going to the movies, Bobby," Black said. "Pam is going to drive them and pick them up when it's over."

"Okay. Have a good time," Bobby said calmly, because Pam had already told him about it.

"Thank you, Daddy," Barbara said in a semi-state of shock.

"That wasn't so bad now, was it?" Rain patted Barbara on the shoulder. "You go on now and finish getting ready." Rain winked at Black and Bobby. "I'll make sure they behave."

"Thanks, Aunt Rain," Barbara said, and went to finish getting ready.

Rain smiled and walked up to Cole. "Bet you thought you was gettin' ready to have a scene from Bad Boys." She laughed. "You know, where Martin Lawrence and Will Smith tease that boy when he came to pick up Martin's daughter. You see that movie?" Rain asked with a big smile on her face.

"Yes, ma'am. It was pretty funny," Cole said and laughed.

Rain stopped laughing and took out her gun. "Well, that ain't Martin Lawrence, and that nigga there *damn sure* ain't no Will Smith. So, if you *even think* about touching Barbara tonight or any other night, I will hunt you down and shoot your little boy dick off. Do you understand me?"

"Yes, ma'am," a very scared Cole said.

"Now you go stand by the front door and wait quietly for Barbara," Rain ordered, and Cole moved away fast. Once he was gone, everybody laughed as Rain came in the living room.

Bobby pointed at Rain. "You a fool," he said.

Black stood up. "Let's go. We got shit to do."

Bobby grabbed his coat and they left the house. Once they were outside, Black told Bobby and Rain what happened to Scarlett, and that Ellis was working for Brill.

"What you wanna do, Mike?" Bobby asked.

"Let's kill them all. Tonight," Black said.

"I like the sound of that." Rain unlocked her car and they got in.

"And I promise, you'll be the one that ends Brill."

"I like the sound of that even better." Rain started up the car and then she drove to her warehouse.

On the way, Black called Sherman and told him they were on their way there and that he needed him to get some men together. Then Black said it again. "This war ends tonight." Then he called Spence and told him to meet them outside Big Mac's.

When Spence got there, Black got out of the car and talked to Spence. Bobby and Rain looked on as Spence listened carefully to what Black had to say, and then he nodded his head and walked toward Big Mac's. Spence took out his phone and called Carolina and told her to come outside.

"I'm working, Spence."

"I know and I'm still asking you to come outside now, so you know it must be important."

"I'll get my coat."

When Carolina came out of the club, she saw Black, Bobby, and Rain get out of the car. Spence walked up to her.

"What's goin' on, Spence?"

"You know Ellis Brock?" Spence asked.

"I know him," Carolina said slowly. "Why?"

"He in there?"

"Yes, he's in there. And I asked you why, Spence?"

"I need you to bring him out, before they go in after him."

"I'm not bringing him out so you can kill him." Carolina turned to go back in the club.

Spence grabbed her and held her by both shoulders. "He beat Black's sister, Carolina. So they're goin' in there

247

and a lot of people might get hurt, or you can bring him out here and nobody gets hurt." Spence let Carolina go. "It's up to you."

"Did he hurt her bad?"

"Yeah, Carolina. He hurt her real bad."

Spence stood and watched as Carolina looked at Black and went back in Big Mac's. Five minutes later, Black saw her coming out with Ellis. She took him to Spence. He and Bobby got in the car and Rain walked across the street to where Spence was standing.

"Spence, this is Ellis Brock," Carolina said quietly and shook her head as she walked away.

"What you want?" Ellis asked.

Rain walked up behind Ellis and put her gun to the base of his skull. "Mike Black wanna talk to you, Ellis."

Spence grabbed Ellis and they took him to Spence's car. Rain got in the backseat with Ellis while Spence got in the front and started the car. Bobby drove Rain's car and Spence followed them to the warehouse.

When they got to the warehouse Sherman, Smoke, Ice, and Mitch were already there, and they watched as Spence dragged Ellis into the warehouse.

"What you got here, Spence?" Sherman asked and then he saw Rain. Black and Bobby weren't far behind her. Spence shoved Ellis toward Black. Black handed Bobby his guns, put on his gloves, and walked toward Ellis.

"So you're Ellis Brock, huh?" Black grabbed him. "My name is Mike Black." He punched Ellis in the face. "I'm your brother-in-law."

Black punched Ellis over and over again in the face.

"I'm gonna beat you to death for touching my sister." Black hit him again. "But before you die, you're gonna tell me where I can find Lloyd Brill tonight." Black reached back and punched him again. This time Ellis went down from the force of the blow.

Black kicked him in the face and then stomped Ellis repeatedly about his head, his shoulders, and his back. Then he grabbed Ellis by his coat and pulled him to his feet. He reached back and hit him again. Black picked Ellis up and threw him to the ground as Jackie came in with Travis.

"What's going on?" Jackie asked Spence.

"That's Black's brother-in-law. He beat Black's sister."

"I didn't know Black had a sister."

"Neither did I," Spence said as Ellis got off the floor and rushed at Black.

Ellis was a big man and strong as hell, but Black was stronger. They struggled for a while and then Black hit Ellis with blow after blow until Ellis went down. Black stood over Ellis and kicked him a few times. Black pulled Ellis up again and rammed him face first into the wall. He slammed Ellis's body into that wall over and over again until Ellis went down. Black stood over him and began to stomp Ellis again.

Everybody in the warehouse stood and watched quietly as Black beat Ellis unmercifully.

Ellis struggled to his feet and came running toward Black. He tackled him and the two of them fell to the ground. Black and Ellis rolled around on the ground for a while exchanging blows. Then Black got on top and hit Ellis several times in the face. He grabbed Ellis by his coat and began pounding Ellis's head into the floor. A pool of blood had formed on the floor by the time Black got off of Ellis. He got to his feet slowly.

By that time Doc, Howard, and Jab had arrived and were watching the beating that Black was dealing Ellis. Howard leaned toward Jackie and asked the same question. "What's going on?" Howard whispered.

"He beat Black's sister."

"I didn't know Black had a sister."

"I don't think anybody knew," Jackie said and watched as the beating continued.

Ellis rushed Black again. Black stepped aside, grabbed Ellis, and rammed him into a wall again. Ellis's face was a bloody mess as Black continued to ram his face into the wall. Black let Ellis go and once again, he slumped to the floor.

Then Black looked around for something to beat Ellis with. He picked up a long piece of metal and stood over Ellis. He tried to cover his head as Black hit him over and over again. Black dropped the metal and pulled Ellis to his feet.

Ellis was dazed; out on his feet, as he swung at him again. Black hit him with lefts and rights to his face, and then threw a punch to the stomach that took all the wind out of Ellis; he collapsed.

Black was out of breath when he picked up an empty 50-gallon drum and dropped it on Ellis. Kayo and Treach got there in time to see Black get on top of Ellis, wrap his hands around Ellis's throat, and choke the shit out of him until he slowly stopped moving and his body went limp and fell to the floor.

"Hey, Black," Sherman yelled. "You forgot to ask him about where to find Brill."

I CAME TO BRING THE PAIN

Everybody in the room laughed, and that included Black.

54

A little later that night, Black, along with Rain, Kayo and Treach arrived at Brill's house. Black and Rain got out of the car and rang the doorbell. One of his bodyguards' opened the door and Black shot him in the forehead. Then he kicked the body out of the way and went inside. Brill's wife, Carissa was in the living room watching television.

"Hello, Carissa," Black said and sat down on the couch next to her.

"Hello, Mike. You gonna kill me?"

"No, Carissa, I'm not gonna kill you," Black said. "But I am gonna burn this house to the ground, so I think that you should go ahead and grab everything you can carry and get outta here."

Carissa stood up. "How much time I got?"

"Not much."

"Okay."

"Carissa."

She stopped and looked at Black. "Yes."

"If Lloyd has any money stashed in the house, I suggest you get that first."

"Please, Mike, I gotta a lotta stuff I gotta take with me."

"You're lucky we go back, Carissa," Black said.

As Rain finished her work, Black made Kayo and Treach help Carissa. In addition to the money Brill had stashed in the house, she took all of her jewelry, as well as her fur coats. When Carissa looked in her shoe closet, Black told her that she was pushing it.

Once they were all out of the house, Rain pressed the detonator and the house blew up.

"Now, Carissa, where's Lloyd?" Black asked.

"He's either at Caribe with Telson or he's with Veatrice," Carissa said as she watched Kayo and Treach put the last of her stuff in her 760Li BMW Sedan.

Barrett Telson, one of Brill's number runners, and his bodyguards Chuck Alford and Eliceo Henry were going to The Caribe Bar & Lounge. They stopped in front to let Telson get out.

"Go with him, Eliceo; make sure he finds his way back," Telson remarked as he got of the car and went inside.

"I'm getting real tired of taking that guys shit," Alford said as he drove away from the door.

"Why don't you just kill him," Henry said as Alford parked the car.

Once they parked Kayo and Treach got out of their car.

"Yeah, and while I'm at it why don't I just shoot Brill and save Black and them the trouble," Alford said as he locked the car.

"You the one that's tired of his shit," Henry said as Kayo and Treach stepped up behind Alford and Henry and shot them once each in the back of their head's.

Black and Rain followed Telson into the restaurant. He was nervous went Black sat down at the table with him. He looked around for his bodyguards, because he was sure that Black was there to kill him.

"I want you to arrange a meeting between me and Brill tonight," Black said as Rain stood behind him. "See if we can't settle our differences."

Then Rain placed the barrel of her gun in Telson's eye. "Fuck you, Black."

Rain pulled the trigger and blew out the back of Telson's head.

At the same time that was happening, Pete Moroder was in a restaurant having dinner with his wife when he saw Bobby and Smoke outside. Knowing that wasn't good, Moroder gave his wife something to powder her nose with and sent her to the bathroom.

Outside the restaurant, Bobby and Smoke moved into position to ambush Moroder when he came out. "You think he saw us?" Smoke asked Bobby.

"Yeah, the mutha fucka saw us. So you go around back in case he comes out that way."

Before Smoke could move to cover the back, Moroder burst through the front door firing and Bobby and Smoke hit him with multiple shots to the head and chest.

Meanwhile, Barry Peters and his enforcer Manny Wynn were coming out of a bar on the avenue, when Ice and Mitch approached them with guns drawn. They pulled their weapons as Ice and Mitch opened fire on them. They hit Peters and Wynn with shots to the head and chest.

While that was happening, Nathan Watts jumped in his car and took off up the block, with Sherman and Doc following behind him. They got in Sherman's Lincoln and went after him.

"Don't lose him, or you'll have to deal with Rain, old man," Doc said and laughed.

"It was your big idea for us to get in the street tonight," Sherman said as he drove.

"And you can't tell me you ain't having fun, Sherman."

"Just like the old days, huh Doc?"

"Yup."

Sherman laughed. "Haven't had this much fun in years."

As Sherman drove, Doc rolled down his window and opened fire on Peters and Wynn until they got to a red light. They returned fire and barreled through the light. As the chase continued Peters and Wynn were overtaken by Sherman and Doc and they riddled their car with bullets. Peters swerved and the car spun out-of-control. Doc kept firing as Peters crashed into a fire hydrant. Then Sherman and Doc got out of the Lincoln and fired on the car and make sure that Peters and Wynn were dead.

Not far away, Bobby and Smoke saw another of Brill's men; James Calloway leaving his building. "Hey, Bobby, ain't that Calloway comin' out the building?"

"Where?" Bobby asked and Smoke slowed down.

"The mutha fucka right there," Smoke said and pointed.

"That's him." Bobby took out his gun. "Let's get him, Smoke."

Smoke pulled over and Bobby got out of the car. "I'll be right back." then Bobby followed Calloway down the street to his car. Smoke watched as Bobby walked up to James Calloway's car and shot him point blank in the head instantly killing him.

Jackie and Travis drove to their target for the evening; George Johnson and Monroe Bellotte. They parked and waited. That night, they had been going from bar to bar drinking. Johnson and Bellotte were drunk as they made their way out of the bar. Not knowing that anybody was after them, they weren't in any particular hurry.

The two drunks made it up the street to the garage where they had parked his car. Bellotte gave the attendant his ticket and waited for the car. When the attendant returned with the car, Johnson and Bellotte jumped in and rolled into the street. They drove down the street and stopped at the red light at the corner. When they did, Jackie and Travis unleashed a barrage of bullets that hit Johnson in the head and killed him, Bellotte was hit in the chest, and abdomen and soon he was dead too.

Early in the morning, Brill, who had spent the night with Veatrice Ferreira, was unaware of what had happened to his organization at Black's hands. That was because everybody that would have normally informed Brill of what was happening was dead.

When Brill walked out of her apartment and got outside, he looked across the street and saw his bodyguard's dead with Black and Rain standing over them. Brill pulled his gun and ran down the steps. When they saw Brill running up the street, Black and Rain opened fire on him.

Black and Rain kept firing at Brill as he ducked behind some cars and kept firing. He stayed low until he got to the corner, then Brill stood up and ran. Firing shots as he ran with Black and Rain in pursuit. Brill reloaded his weapon and fired on them. With Black and Rain behind him firing shots, Brill ran up to a building with guns blazing and then he ran inside.

"He's all yours," Black said.

Rain ran toward the house and ran up the stairs after him. She kicked opened the door and went in. Rain looked up and saw Brill on the steps; she ducked in the shadows as he opened fire. As Brill ran up the steps, Rain returned fire. She got to her feet and followed Brill up the steps.

Rain moved quickly and quietly through the building, guns drawn, looking for Brill. When Rain heard footsteps coming toward her, she got out of sight and waited. It was just a man on his way to work. Once he passed, Rain continued her search. Now that she had checked that floor, Rain made her way up the steps.

When Rain heard more footsteps coming, Rain stepped into the shadows and pointed her guns. Rain waited until they passed. "More people going to work."

Rain watched as they stopped at the elevator and talked. Rain hoped the elevator wouldn't be long for fear that Brill might get away. Once the elevator came and they were out of sight, Rain came out of the shadows and continued her search. Rain walked down the hallway until she thought she saw movement. Rain picked up an empty can and tossed it in that direction.

Brill stood up, spread his arms, and fired in both directions at once.

Rain laughed at how she had him.

Brill didn't wait around to see if he hit anything, he ran for the steps and went up. Rain ran up the steps after Brill; she took aim, and fired one of her guns until it was empty. Brill fired back at Rain and went up another flight. As Rain ran up the steps, she reloaded her weapon. When she reached the top of the stairs, Rain shot back.

Brill continued running up the steps, busting shots as he reached the door to the roof. He shot the lock and went out on the roof. Knowing that Rain was right behind him, Brill turned and fired several shots through the door. Rain pressed her back against the wall and stayed still until the shooting stopped. Then she opened the door and stepped out, but she didn't see Brill anywhere. Just then, Brill came out of hiding and opened fired at Rain and she fired back at him.

Now Brill was out of bullets.

Brill started backing up and begging Rain not to kill him. As she reloaded her weapon, Rain kept coming at Brill and he kept backing up until he got to the edge. He stopped and looked over his shoulder and almost fell off the roof.

When Black looked up from the street and saw Brill on the edge, he decided that it might be a good idea to move. "Just in case."

Back up on the roof, Brill dropped to his knees as Rain approached him.

"Please don't kill me," Brill pleaded. "I got money. I could pay you whatever you want."

Rain laughed. "If you talkin' 'bout the money you had hid in your house; your wife took that before I burned the bitch to the ground."

"Damn."

"I'm gonna shoot you now, just like you did my daddy."

"Come on, Rain, give me a fuckin' break. That was years ago and besides, that was business."

"Yeah well, that was my daddy you shot and that shit was personal to me, so all that business shit went out the fuckin' window. You should've killed me when I was born."

Rain put one in the chamber.

"I was gonna give you the same chance you gave my daddy. You remember, you shot him and left him to die. But that shit is too good for you."

I CAME TO BRING THE PAIN

Rain raised her weapon and emptied her clip.

55

And then there was peace.

With Lloyd Brill, Rob Berry, and Gee Cameron all dead, and Hector's people moving into the areas that were once controlled by Nado Benitez, things were slowly returning to some semblance of order. It had been a couple of days since Rain killed Brill, and during that time, nobody had had to fire a single shot.

Now that it was over, Black, Bobby, and Rain got together in Bobby's office at Impressions to have a drink to celebrate the end of Wanda's war. They had finished one round and Bobby was just about to pour everybody another, when there was a knock at the door. When Bobby looked and saw that it was Tara, he pressed the button to allow her in.

"Sorry to bother you, Bobby, but there is an FBI Agent"—Tara looked at the card in her hand—"McCullough, asking to see you."

"He asked for Bobby by name?" Black asked.

"Yes, and it's a woman."

Bobby snapped his fingers. "That's the agent that was working with Dawson."

"Show her in," Black said, and Tara left the office.

"Lanisha told me that she was the one who used to wire her up," Bobby said after Tara left.

"What do you think she wants?" Rain asked.

Tara knocked at the door.

"Guess we're about to find out," Black said, and Bobby pressed the button.

Tara opened the door and escorted the agent in. "FBI Agent Bridgette McCullough," she introduced, and then Tara left the office.

"Mike Black, Bobby Ray, and Rain Robinson; I wasn't expecting all three of you to be here, but I'm glad you are."

"Have a seat, Agent McCullough. Tell us what we can do for you?" Bobby asked.

"Thank you." Agent McCullough sat down. "And it's what we can do for each other."

"Can I offer you a drink, Agent McCullough?"

"Johnnie Red, straight up."

While Bobby fixed the agent her drink, Rain stared at Agent McCullough. She was staring at Black. He sipped his drink and looked unconcerned by the agent's presence in the office, but he was concerned, very concerned. As Bobby handed the agent her drink, Black wanted to know what she wanted and wasted no time asking.

"What do you want?"

"Mike Black. Straight to the point. Just like I expected." McCullough sipped her drink. "First, I want to say what an honor it is to meet you all." She raised her glass. "And I want to congratulate you on defeating your enemies."

Agent McCullough took a sip, but she drank alone.

"Rob Berry, Gee Cameron, and Lloyd Brill are all dead," Agent McCullough paused, "And convincing Hector Villanueva to step back into the New York market was pure genius."

Agent McCullough sipped her drink to the sound of silence.

"You still haven't answered my question," Black said.

"What I want is to show you something." Agent McCullough took a large envelope out and handed the contents to Bobby.

There were two pictures. One of Black, Bobby, and Rain going into a building; and another of them coming out of the building.

"This supposed to mean something?" Bobby asked as he handed the pictures to Black.

"Note the date and time stamp." Black handed the pictures to Rain. "They were taken on the night that Cynt Platt was killed. The building the three of you are going into is where Lee Gilbert and Titus Wallace were killed. Medical examiner marked the time of death as being between two-thirty and three-thirty a.m. If you look at the time stamp on those pictures, you'll see why somebody might conclude that you killed those men."

Black laughed and then he stood up. He looked at the agent, and then he went to the bar and poured himself a drink. "Since everybody in this room knows that you're not here to arrest us, I'll ask you one more time. What do you want Agent McCullough?"

"To give you those pictures," Agent McCullough reached in her pocket, "and this."

Black nodded his head and Rain got up and took the memory card from the agent.

"That's where those pictures are. There are no copies."

Rain handed the card to Bobby and he inserted the card in his computer. Once he had verified that the images were on there, he nodded at Black.

"Destroy it," Black said and then he reclaimed his seat. Now he was sure that he knew exactly what the agent wanted.

"Now I'm really curious," Bobby said as he put the card in an ashtray and set it on fire. "What the fuck you want?"

"I come to offer you my services."

"What fuckin' service is that?" Rain asked.

"Information. I let you know when unfortunate things are about to happen. Would that be worth something to you?"

Rain glanced at Black and he nodded. "What would be a far more useful to us would be preventive services," she said.

"That wouldn't be a problem either. You'll find that I can provide you with a wide range of services. Services that you could offer to others for a fee."

"Do you mind waiting outside while we talk about this, Agent McCullough?" Rain asked.

"Not a problem." McCullough stood up and left the office.

"What you wanna do, Mike?" Bobby asked as soon as the door closed.

"You want me to kill her?" Rain volunteered.

"Why?" Black asked.

"Because she's got us," Bobby said.

"No, Bobby, we have her." Black smiled. "Let her in, Rain."

Rain opened the door and let the agent in the office. Once the agent had reclaimed her seat, Black got up and poured her another shot of Johnnie Red. He handed it to her.

"I think we can do business, Agent McCullough."

She smiled. "Agent McCullough sounds so formal with us being partners and all. You can call me B Mon'e."

56
Freeport, Grand Bahama Island

With Wanda's war behind them, Black and Shy returned to Freeport to relax and spend some time with their children. Black's mother, M, prepared a welcome home dinner feast that was fit for a King and his queen. Jerk marinated steak and chicken, rice and peas, shrimp skewers, oxtail with broad beans, beef patties, conch fritters, fried plantains, spinach soup, and fruit cake for dessert.

The following day, Black and Shy took the family to the Garden of the Groves. "This is one of the first places your father took me when we began dating," Shy told her children. "Your father was quite the romantic."

Black looked at Shy, she looked at him.

Napoleon looked at them; he had seen that look before and it let him know it was going to be an early night for them. He looked at M, she shook her head. "Come on, children," M said and led the children away with Napoleon following closely behind.

Black and Shy stood there looking at each other. "We should catch up with them," Black said slowly as they continued to stare into one another's eyes.

"We should." Then Shy eased her hand in his and they walked away hand in hand.

The first time they visited the Garden of the Groves, Black and Shy spent the day strolling around and enjoying its tranquility. This time, they took one of the guided tours. Their guide shared her knowledge of the flora and fauna of the Garden, as well as the birdlife. She gave the children a glimpse into the history of the Garden and the island, and introduced them to the unique fresh water resource.

Since it was somewhat more protected from the wind and waves than Taino Beach or Lucaya Beach, they spent the rest of the day at Xanadu Beach. The water is shallow, so it's a good place to take small children who can't swim. That afternoon, Black and Shy went snorkeling on a small coral reef out near the end of the breakwater.

Later that evening, and after the children had gone to bed, Black and Shy retired to their room for the evening. Shy opened the French doors to allow the warm Caribbean breeze to fill the room. When she got in the bed, Shy knew that she would cum from his slightest touch, because she had wanted him all day.

Black slid his hand across her chest, admiring the softness of her skin, before taking one of Shy's nipples into his mouth. Shy leaned back against the headboard and held Black's head in place with one hand, and squeezed her breast with the other. Shy took his face into her hands and kissed him gently. Their kiss was long, tender, and his tongue felt like it was overpowering hers; bending her to his will. Shy gladly submitted.

Black looked at Shy. To him, she was still the most beautiful woman that he had ever known, and he loved her with every fiber of his being. Shy got on her knees and ran her hand over Black's body. She started from his ankles; along his leg to his thighs. Then Shy stroked him and felt him getting harder in her hand. Once his dick was rock hard, Shy smiled and began running her tongue around the head. He looked down at Shy as she ran her tongue along the sides of his shaft. Shy stroked Black and then she took him into her mouth.

Then Black crawled between Shy's legs and very deliberately spread her lips with his thumb and forefinger, while making small circles around her clit with the tip of his finger. Black rubbed her swollen clit. Shy was drenched from all that he was making her feel. There were no words that could describe the sensation that she felt when Black slid his tongue inside of her and sucked her moist lips gently. Shy felt her body quiver as Black licked her clit with the tip of his tongue, weaving magic that she felt at her core. Shy's head drifted back as the circles he made built the tension inside before making her explode. Shy's thighs pressed together as her body convulsed uncontrollably.

Black laid there next to Shy; she began gliding her hand up and down his erection. Shy got up on the bed and eased herself down on it. She moaned her pleasure while continuing to slide up and down his shaft. The feeling got her so caught up that Shy screamed his name while she slammed her body against his in anxious anticipation of each stroke. Determined to bring them both to climax together, she rode him harder; working her hips and inner muscles until he couldn't hold back any longer. When he began to swell and exploded inside of her, Shy screamed his name again and collapsed on his chest.

Early the next morning, Black opened his eyes and looked over at Shy. She was still asleep and had a very satisfied smile on her face. He eased out of bed quietly, got dressed and left the room. When he got to the kitchen, he found Napoleon seated at the table and his mother at the stove cooking chicken souse, and grits 'n tuna for Napoleon to eat. M had already served him corned beef 'n grits with hot red pepper, and eggs and Bahamian Johnny cakes to eat.

"Good morning, Michael," M said when she saw him come in.

"Morning, Ma," Black said and kissed his mother on the cheek.

"Morning, Boss," Napoleon said with his mouth full.

"Happy now?" Black asked Napoleon.

Napoleon nodded his head as he continued to chew his food.

"I can't tell you how much he missed your cooking," Black said as he sat down at the table.

"He said Cassandra was trying to starve him to death," M said. "I love Cassandra like she was the daughter I never had, but for the life of me, I just don't know how you married a woman that can't cook."

"Believe me, Ma; Cassandra has other very appealing qualities."

"I don't need to know all that, Michael." M shook her head. "You want some breakfast?"

"I'll have what he's having. Just not as much and no grits, please." Black turned to Napoleon. "After we eat, I wanna make that run."

"As I felt that you might. I have the car gassed up and ready to go. I have also made arrangements for a boat to take us there."

"Good man," Black said as M placed a plate in front of him.

After breakfast, Napoleon drove Black out of Freeport on the Grand Bahama Highway until it ended. Then they boarded the boat that Napoleon had chartered, and set sail for Big Cross Cay. Once they were docked, Napoleon secured a car and drove Black out the coastal highway until they reached a property consisting of three-and-a-half acres, uniquely situated between the ocean and the bay that enjoyed both a dazzling beach frontage and a serene bay frontage.

The house was three thousand square feet of living space with five bedrooms, and five full and two partial baths. The house incorporated a casual living room, refreshingly bright dining room, and a well-equipped kitchen overlooking an aquamarine pool, set against a stunning Bahamian backdrop.

Black and Napoleon approached the door and rang the bell. It took a minute, but when the door finally was opened, Keisha Orr was standing there. She was wearing a sheer 6 Shore Road Miles cover-up, trimmed with colorful embroidery, which she had tied loosely across her chest. It did little to hide Keisha's stunning body in the halter bikini with high-waisted cutout bikini bottoms that she had on under it.

"Morning, Mr. Black," Keisha said and she allowed him in the house.

"Good morning, Keisha."

"You coming in, Napoleon, or are you just going to stand there with your mouth open?" Keisha asked.

"I am coming inside, Keisha. But I must say that you look exceptional today."

"Thank you, Napoleon."

"How's she doing?" Black asked.

"She's good today."

"Where is she?"

"Out on the deck."

"Thanks," Black said as Napoleon made himself comfortable in the living room.

Black went out on the deck. There he found Wanda reclining in a deck chair, wearing a Badgley Mischka Fiona Caftan, and sipping coffee. "When I heard the bell ring, I knew it had to be you." Wanda laughed. "Especially since nobody ever comes here."

Black kissed her on the cheek. "How are you, Wanda?" he asked and sat down next to her.

"I feel good today, Mike," Wanda said, and Black thought back to the night that Wanda got shot.

Black stood over Wanda and Keisha as Bobby walked up. Keisha was holding Wanda and trying to stop the bleeding. Black and Bobby looked at each other and then down at Wanda. Then Bobby took out his phone and called Perry.

"How is she?"

"I don't know, but there's a lot of blood," Bobby said.

"I don't think I can get to Cuisine in time, Bobby. You got to call 9-1-1. Wanda surviving this is going to depend on how quickly she gets to a hospital."

Bobby looked at Black and told him what Perry said, and Black got on the phone.

"Can we move her at all?"

"I would not move her unless her safety is in jeopardy. In the meantime, follow basic first aid procedures. Be sure to keep her airway open and clear, and try to control any bleeding. Where is she hit?"

"In the stomach on her right side," Black said.

"That's not good. An abdominal wound generally needs major surgery to fix the injuries to the intestines and other abdominal organs that may also be injured. There are also some major vessels that can be injured. Infection is a major potential problem. If her stomach ruptures, then she has about fifteen minutes before acid enters her bloodstream. I know you don't want to do it, Mike, but you gotta call 9-1-1 or Wanda will die."

"I understand." Black looked at Keisha. "Let Bobby do that, Keisha. I need you to call 9-1-1."

"You're doing the right thing, Mike," Perry said.

"Yeah. Anything else I need to do?"

"Just keep her comfortable until the ambulance gets there. And don't elevate her legs. Gunshot wounds to the abdomen will bleed more quickly once the legs are elevated, and that will make it harder for her to breathe. Call me back and let me know what hospital you take her to, and I'll meet you there."

"I got it." Black ended the call.

"They're on their way," Keisha said.

"We need to take her outside, Bobby," Black said.

"Definitely don't want the cops up in here," Bobby said as Keisha resumed applying pressure to Wanda's wound.

"I'm sorry, but we have to move you outside, Wanda."

Wanda grimaced in pain and nodded her head. With that, Black and Bobby picked Wanda up and carried her outside and laid her down outside of Cuisine. The ambulance came ten minutes later. After surgery, the doctor came out and talked to Keisha and Perry.

"She's going to be fine. The shot went in through the side of the abdomen. The bullet passed through the muscles surrounding the abdomen, and never entered the abdominal cavity."

Shortly thereafter, Napoleon arrived at the hospital; and he got Wanda out of there and took her to the Westchester County Airport to meet Black.

"Did we get everything on?"

"Yes, Boss. All of our cargo is secure," Napoleon said that night. "And I have some people in place to meet us at the plane. They will take care of things from there."

"Good man."

Once they arrived in Freeport, Napoleon waited until Black's family was off the plane and had left the airport, before he allowed the men to take Wanda and Keisha off the plane. Then they took them to the house in Big Cross Cay, where Wanda was able to rest and recover.

"I'm glad you're feeling better, Wanda."

"So, what's going on back in the world?" she asked.

"The war you started is over. Lloyd Brill, Rob Berry, and Gee Cameron are dead."

"What about Benitez?"

"I killed him that same night he shot you."

"What about Nina; is she all right?"

"In Aruba with Leon."

"I know she must be bored to death," Wanda said. "I know I am."

Black didn't comment for a while. For the next ten minutes they sat in silence and stared out at the Caribbean Sea.

"What the fuck were you thinking, Wanda?"

"I was thinking that we needed to control everything, Mike. Not some of it, all of it."

"You took us to war and a lot of good people—our people—died."

Collateral damage, Wanda thought but didn't say. "I'm sorry about that, Mike, I really am. But this was the right move. Sooner or later, they would have come after us."

Black shook his head, knowing that there was a part of him that knew that Wanda was right. As Rob Berry and Gee Cameron got bigger and stronger, they would have made a move against Black. And the fact was that, even though they had existed peacefully with Lloyd Brill for years, he had always coveted their operation. But Black was still so mad at Wanda for what she had done, that he couldn't see beyond that. He loved Wanda; she was as much his sister as Bobby was his brother. Black looked at Wanda.

Which is the only reason you're still alive.

"What did you do about their drug business?"

"I convinced Hector to step back in to the New York market."

Wanda turned to Black and smiled. "See, Mike, except for Hector stepping in to take Nina's spot, it all worked out the way I planned it."

Once again, there was a long silence between them.

"When do you think that I can come home, Mike?" Wanda asked.

"I don't know."

58

Atlanta, Georgia

Marcus Douglas drove down I-20 heading downtown. His oldest client, Richard "Rabbit" Seville, had been arrested over the weekend and was charged with double homicide. He was accused of killing his wife, Tiara, and his girlfriend, Kyra Warthen. Marcus had an appointment to meet in Judge Brewer's chambers to discuss the case with the ADA.

On the way there, Marcus thought back to the first day that he opened his private practice. He hadn't even finished unloading the car, when Kim Seville walked in the door. Marcus put down the box he was carrying and wiped his hands. "Can I help you, ma'am?" he said as he walked toward her.

"I need to see the lawyer."

"My name is Marcus Douglas." He smiled and extended his hand, feeling good about having his first client and he hadn't even finished unpacking. "Go ahead and have a seat. Can I get you anything?"

"No, thank you. I just need to see the lawyer."

Marcus sat down at the desk. "What can I do for you?"

"You're the lawyer?"

"Yes, ma'am."

"Really?" She smiled.

"Yes, ma'am. Tell me what I can do for you?"

Mrs. Seville explained that her nineteen-year-old son, Richard, had gotten arrested coming out of the weed house. "How much was he caught with?"

"They didn't catch no drugs on Rabbit," Mrs. Seville said.

"Who's Rabbit?"

Mrs. Seville laughed a little. "That's just what we call Richard."

"Then what did they arrest him for?"

"Resisting arrest."

It didn't take long for Marcus to arrange bail and get him out. When he talked to Rabbit, he told Marcus that after the police searched him and didn't find any drugs or money, they wouldn't let him leave. "Why?" Marcus asked.

"That's what I asked them and I started walking away. Then the cop grabbed me and told me I was under arrest."

When it went to court, Marcus got the case dismissed, since Rabbit didn't have any drugs on him. However, there was a reason why Rabbit wasn't caught with any drugs on him. That was because Rabbit wasn't there to buy drugs; it was his weed spot. At the age of nineteen, Rabbit had begun building his drug empire and was about to enter the cocaine market. Now Rabbit was thirty-two and he had product and people moving it in Georgia, Alabama, Florida, North and South Carolina. But now he was in trouble again.

When Marcus arrived at the Fulton County Courthouse on Pryor Street and parked in the lot, he rushed to Judge Brewer's chambers. When he arrived at the judge's chambers, Marcus was met by Assistant District Attorney Izella Hawkins. "Morning, Izella."

"Good Morning, Marcus."

"I just want you to know that I've filed a formal motion to dismiss for lack of evidence, Izella. You don't have a case."

"You're right, we don't."

"Then I hope you won't oppose me in chambers the way you usually do."

"That's because I enjoy sparing with you." Izzella laughed. "You're still the only real challenge I get around here these days."

"Your fault for being an excellent prosecutor."

Izzella let out a little giggle. "Maybe I shouldn't prepare for a case; just go in and wing it."

"That's one way to level the playing field," Marcus paused. "I'm serious, Izzella. Mr. Seville didn't kill those women."

"Mr. Seville." Izella shook her head. "I don't know how you defend that guy."

"He was my first client. Back in those days, his retainer paid the rent for the first few months. I've tried to pass him off to another lawyer on my staff, but he won't have any of it."

"I understand you being loyal to him, but he's the worst kind of scum."

"Even the worst kind of scum deserves a quality defense."

"True."

"Truth is, the facts just don't fit the crime."

"I know that, Marcus. I looked it over—remember me, Ms. Preparation? I know that the arresting officers shouldn't have charged Mr. Seville. But why don't you tell me his story."

"He says that him and his wife, Tiara, were upstairs in bed, when they heard a loud noise downstairs. Mr. Seville got up to investigate and found that Kyra Warthen had broken a window and had entered the residents."

"And she was his girlfriend, right?"

"Right."

"Go on."

"Mr. Seville and Ms. Warthen begin arguing, and at some point, his wife Tiara hears the argument and comes downstairs. Mr. Seville said that when Ms. Warthen saw his wife; she pulled out a gun and shot her. At this point, Mr. Seville makes a grab for the gun. They wrestle for the gun and it accidently discharges, killing Ms. Warthen. GSR tests were conducted on both Mr. Seville and Ms. Warthen's clothing and skin. There was residue on the gloves Ms. Warthen was wearing and on her clothes. However, only traces of residue were found on Mr. Seville's clothes, and there wasn't any detected on his hands. Since we know that gunshot residue can travel anywhere from three to five feet from the gun, I think it is safe to conclude that is how the residue got on his clothes. And I think the judge will agree that Ms. Warthen's death was accidental."

Marcus was right; the judge agreed with him and the charges against Mr. Seville were dropped. After the case was dismissed and he was released from custody, Rabbit went to the house of another girlfriend, Holly Morgan. He parked his car and approached the house. When he passed the living room window, Rabbit stopped in his tracks when he looked in and saw Holly's body lying in a pool of blood. Rabbit took out his cell and called Marcus.

"How does it feel to be a free man, Rabbit?" Marcus asked when he answered.

"Great," Rabbit said as he walked away from the house. "But that ain't why I called."

"What's up?"

I CAME TO BRING THE PAIN

"I just got to a friend of mines house and I can see her lying on the floor," Rabbit got in his car and started it up. "I think she's dead, Marcus."

"Did you call 9-1-1?"

"No. I'm getting the fuck away from here. I just got out of jail. I ain't trying to go right back."

"Rabbit, I want you to listen to me. Hang up with me and call 9-1-1. The last thing you need is for one of her nosey neighbors to say they saw you leaving the scene. So call the police, now, Rabbit. I'm on my way to you."

"I'll be the one in handcuffs when you get here."

THE END OF I CAME TO BRING THE PAIN

ROY GLENN

The Mike Black Saga
continues in
It's A New Day

JUL 1 0 2015

CPSIA information can be obtained at www.ICGtesting.com
Printed in the USA
LVOW04s1436180615

442982LV00018B/586/P

9 781514 238752